MURDER

— AT —

KNEBWORTH

A Historical Mystery Novel

CHARLES W. SNYDER

For Sylvia

and

In Memory of Rupert

CHAPTER ONE

A DINNER AT ROCKBRIDGE HOUSE, LONDON

December, 1868

Never before in her young life had Marie Deflorette been so gloriously enthralled as she was that evening at Lord Burnley's dinner party at Rockbridge House, Park Lane. Although in years past, she had dined at some of the finest homes in Charleston and Wilmington, she had seen nothing that compared to the Rockbridge dining room. She couldn't resist gazing at the gorgeous crystal chandelier that illuminated the wonderful white wainscoting and the blue willow china that adorned the table. Candlelight played off the brilliant family portraits on the walls. Marie particularly admired the portrait of a figure in ermine robes and bewigged in eighteenth-century style. Lord Burnley had identified the man as his great-grandfather, and the artist as Gainsborough. Or did he say Reynolds? Marie always mixed up those two.

Although she prided herself on being a good listener (her husband Philip insisted on that quality in his wife), Marie was finding it difficult to pay attention to anything she was told. Everything was just so exciting. Whenever Lord Burnley (Lord Burnley!) introduced her to other guests, it seemed each one of them had a title of some sort. It was Lord this or Lady that, and the words "Lord" or "Lady" so arrested Marie's mind that she heard nothing that followed. What Marie gleaned from each introduction was that it meant she had arrived. At long last, little Marie from Wilmington, North Carolina, was taking her rightful place among the cream of the English aristocracy. Why, she thought, the only one here lacking some sort of title, besides herself and Philip, was Philip's employer, Mark Hornell; but she believed Mark stood so high in the realm of political journalism that he might justly be ranked as an aristocrat himself, and, as for Philip, he, of course, was one of nature's noblemen.

As the dinner progressed, Marie began to worry that she was being uncharacteristically silent and unsociable, so wrapped up in her own thoughts. She glanced across the table at the fat, red-faced, middle-aged man seated opposite her. She tried to remember what Lord Burnley had said when he introduced her to him earlier that evening, but all she could recall was an impression that the man was someone important! Perhaps he had been a formidable soldier: something about his close-cropped hair and thick neck called to mind images of marching men and the sound of drums.

Marie's glance then moved from the plump gentleman to the even plumper lady seated to his right—no doubt his wife, Lady something! Her Ladyship appeared delighted to chat with Philip, seated just to her right. Marie could hear little of what they were saying, but she knew from experience that Philip was being very charming as only a practiced diplomat can be. The same conversational skill that had served him so well as an agent of the now defunct Confederate States of America would no doubt make for a memorable evening for the matronly wife of a ruddy old soldier. What a shame, Marie thought, that Philip might be denied the important career to which his talents entitled him. He obviously could not become a British diplomat, nor could he yet safely return to the reunited United States.

All the same, Marie was happy to remain in England and never more so than at that dinner at Rockbridge House. She was so grateful to Mark for making it possible. She decided she had better try being more sociable, and she tried to strike up a conversation with the gentleman seated to her right. She thought him a most good-looking young man, with abundant blond hair and brilliant blue eyes. Certainly, his clothes—sky-blue jacket and pearl-grey waistcoat—were of the height of fashion. But he had an annoying habit of turning his gaze toward the ceiling while Marie was speaking to him, which caused her to chatter excessively as she tried to regain his attention. She was also annoyed by the way his lips would curl as he spoke, as if he thought himself a most superior person, who would condescend to favor one by saying even a few words. No, Marie thought, he's nowhere near as handsome as Philip, nor nearly as nice. She let the conversation lapse, and the young man turned back to the lady seated to his right, evidently his wife, who addressed him as Henry. The name jogged Marie's memory, and she recalled that Lord Burnley had earlier introduced the young man as Lord Henry Worthing. He thinks he's the smartest person in the room, Marie thought, but he's not.

Marie began to look longingly across the table at Philip, who was deep in conversation with the soldier's stout wife. My goodness, Marie thought, how handsome Philip looks in his new suit, with his brown hair neatly parted in the middle, long enough to flow over his right ear and nearly over his left ear as well. Whatever he was saying must have been most amusing.

Certainly, the soldier's lady seemed to be having the time of her life.

Marie's attention was then diverted to the rather elderly gentleman seated to her left. She had not caught his name when they were introduced earlier, except of course that it included the word Lord. She did remember that much. Now, as his Lordship was having a few quiet words with Mark, Marie began to study the face of the older man. He wore a well-trimmed mustache and chin whiskers, as well as abundant sideburns that extended to the jaw line. Although his face appeared to be that of a man over 60 years of age, neither the mustache nor the whiskers betrayed even a trace of gray. His most distinctive feature was his aquiline nose that made one think of the noblest of Romans. But what struck Marie was that his face, in repose, seemed to her the saddest face she had ever seen.

Mark soon wrapped up what had evidently been a confidential conversation between them by saying, "Certainly, Lord Lytton, I'll attend to it at once." "Lord Lytton!" Marie repeated in an involuntarily loud voice. The older man turned to her and slightly bowed his head in acknowledgment. "Lord Lytton," Marie continued, "it is such an honor to meet you." He bowed again, this time allowing a slight smile to brighten his countenance. "It's a greater honor," Marie added, "to dine alongside the author of The Caxtons than to dine with … oh, even than to dine with the Prince of Wales!

Why, where I come from, everybody who's anybody has read The Last Days of Pompeii."

"Thank you. I admire your literary taste, as well as that of your compatriots. But, my dear, just where do you come from?"

"Why, from a long, long way away. Originally from Charleston, South Carolina. You may not know the place, but believe me, everyone there knows you. Charleston is a great center of art and literature."

"Most gratifying. But, if my recollection does not fail me, it was precisely there that the late American War commenced. Were you indeed an eyewitness to those momentous events?"

"Why, Lord Lytton, I was so young at the time, I scarcely can remember. I do believe that at about that time, I had moved up to Wilmington. Do you know Wilmington, North Carolina? Anyway, I know nothing of politics and care less. Now, Wilmington's a wonderful place 'cause that's where I met and married my Philip. There's my husband seated right over there."

Lytton shifted his gaze for a moment toward the slightly startled young man seated across the table from him and then resumed the conversation with Marie.

"Yes, I had the pleasure of being introduced by Lord Burnley to Mr. Deflorette earlier this evening, and we enjoyed a brief but enlightening conversation. Mr. Deflorette is assuredly a gentleman of distinction."

That remark elicited a derisive snort from Lord Henry Worthing that Marie pointedly ignored.

"Don't you agree, Lord Lytton," she asked, "that Philip is just ever so handsome?"

"My dear Mrs. Deflorette, I, of course, cannot know what emotions your husband's visage may inspire in those of your sex, but, since meeting you, I know only too well what envy he arouses in those of my own."

The remark both disconcerted and embarrassed Marie, who had never thought of herself as beautiful. Despite her uneasiness, she thanked Lytton for the compliment. She decided it would be best to turn the conversation, which at this point had the attention of everyone around the table.

"I want to apologize, Lord Lytton, for my disparaging remark earlier about politics. I just remembered that, in addition to being a great novelist, you have devoted yourself to politics as well."

"No apology needed, my dear. It is no matter. Since I was elevated to the House of Lords a couple of years ago, I have removed myself from active political life and, I own, it is a great relief to be done with it. Still, I retain great interest in the course of events."

"Were you much saddened that Mr. Disraeli is being replaced as Prime Minister by Mr. Gladstone? I do believe I read somewhere that you once served in the Cabinet with Mr. Disraeli."

"Quite true, my dear. A decade ago, I held the office of Colonial Secretary under Lord Derby, while Disraeli served as Chancellor of the Exchequer and Leader of the House of Commons. But my acquaintance with Dizzy—I mean Mr. Disraeli—goes back long years before that.

"We met when we were mere youths—both of us scribbling novels about the haut monde, a world we hardly knew ourselves. We read each other's books. He would praise mine, and I would criticize his. It was a most satisfactory arrangement."

"Did you ever imagine back then that he would one day become Prime Minister?" Marie asked, exhilarated at the prospect of being in the know.

"Certainly not," Lytton responded. "Except that, on one occasion, I did in fact divine it. As some of you may know," he added, looking around the table, "I have, through much study of antique volumes, acquainted myself with the mysteries of geomancy, the ancient Arabic practice of foretelling the future from patterns of sand. Years ago, I used that method to tell Disraeli his fortune, and the sands revealed that he would one day hold the highest office and be much honored. So, you see, my skill as a geomancer exceeded my own judgment of men."

At the mention of geomancy, Lady Henry Worthing realized that Lord Henry was about to launch some sarcasm that would give offense to the distinguished novelist, and she jumped into the conversation before her husband could say a word.

"Now that we're on the subject of politics," she said in a voice loud enough to discourage interruption, "I have a question for you. You see, I have no intention of missing this opportunity to discuss politics with gentlemen who really know the subject. On too many occasions, the subject is not broached until we ladies have withdrawn." All the while, as she continued stating her complaint about how the men kept mum about affairs of state until they were enjoying their brandy and cigars after the ladies had left, Lady Henry Worthing was trying to think of an appropriate question to ask. At last, it came to her.

"Lord Lytton, you spoke a moment ago about your judgment of men. Tell us, please, what is your judgment of Mr. Gladstone now that he is Prime Minister?"

The question evidently pleased Lytton, for he smiled broadly for the first time that evening.

"Mr. Gladstone is also an old friend of mine," he began. "He entered Parliament about 35 years ago, not long after I first took my seat there. At the time, I was quite a Radical, while Gladstone was very much on the other side. In fact, Macaulay, my late and very much-lamented friend of Cambridge days, described Gladstone as 'the rising hope of the stern and unbending Tories.' Now, all these years later, I'm the Tory and he the Radical—or, if you prefer the modern term, a

Liberal." Lytton stretched out the word "Liberal," giving emphasis to each syllable.

"For quite some time, you know, Gladstone remained on the fence between the two parties. When I was Colonial Secretary, I sent him on a mission to Corfu in the Greek Isles that were then under the British flag. The task entrusted to him was as complex as the Gordian knot, and Gladstone proved to be no Alexander. Still, I suppose he did as well as could be expected. Perhaps the same will prove true of his premiership."

"Well, I, for one, hold out no hope for him," the stout soldier interjected, "unless he can put down these Fenian insurrectionists, like the ones that blew up Clerkenwell Prison last year. I suspect there are plenty more like that, lurking in dark alleys."

"How true, Sir William," Philip said in his soothing voice. "That explosion was indeed an outrage, so many innocent people killed."

Lytton shook his head. "Such matters are not for the Prime Minister. They fall within the purview of the Home Secretary. Mark, who is to have the Home Office in the new Ministry?"

"It's up in the air," Mark responded. "The chap tipped for it lost his seat, and they're searching for another constituency for him."

"All that's quite true," Lord Burnley agreed. "But Gladstone is taking on the problem in his own way. He has said his mission is to pacify Ireland. If he can do that, we'll have no more trouble from insurrectionists."

Lytton shook his head again. "Gladstone will find Ireland an even knottier problem than the Greek Isles." Turning to Marie, he added in a kindly tone, "I hope we've not been boring you with all this talk of politics."

"Not at all. I know I really should take an interest in it."

"What are the subjects in which you do take an interest, my dear?"

"Well, literature, of course. I love to read. And, if I say so myself, I'm pretty handy with my knitting needles."

"Marie's just being modest," Philip said with a smile. "She's actually an accomplished musician, and she sings charmingly."

That revelation impressed Lytton, who began to think he had underestimated his pretty dinner companion.

"My dear Marie, you should never deny your gift nor let it go to waste. Especially such a gift as a beautiful voice that enchains and entrances with harmonies that reveal the even greater beauty that resides within your very soul."

"Lord Lytton, you very kindly give me too much credit. I do love music; I admit just that much. I can't remember a time when I couldn't play the piano. As for singing, I've been fortunate to have had some fine teachers. Thanks to them, I can at least sing on key. Trouble is, I dislike performing in public—I mean, before a large audience. My dream is not to perform in some great theater but to compose music. That's what I'd love to be—a composer."

"A dream, indeed," Lord Henry said in his sardonic way. "In all the annals of music, there never has been a woman composer worth tuppence."

Across the table, the portly soldier Sir William Carey spoke up. "Nonsense. Man or woman, it makes no difference."

"Thank you, sir," Marie said, smiling. She thought, perhaps Sir William is not such a martinet after all.

"No," Sir William continued, "the problem is, there's only so many notes, only so many sounds, and only so many ways of arranging them. The scientific fact is that, by this late date, practically all the music that can be written has been written."

"I cannot believe that to be so," Marie said, with unexpected firmness. "Nearly all the time, I hear music in my head. Sometimes, I'm not sure if it's music I've heard performed somewhere or music I'm making up myself. Someday, I'll write down the notes and find out if it's something original and all mine."

"Brava!" Lytton enthused. "My dear, you think as all true artists do." Looking around the table and then directly at Sir William, he added, "I appreciate your viewpoint, but I do not share it. I fear you underestimate the creative capacity of artistic genius. But I, artist in words, and young Marie, budding artist in music, feel at once a bond of mutual sympathy and respect. Our true nature is in our thoughts. As artists, we delight in the creations of our imagination, whether or not we inscribe them and place them before the public."

"Don't know that I can follow all that," Sir William responded. "I was just trying to spare the young lady a lot of disappointment. Of course, I wish her well if she wants to try it."

Lytton then addressed Sir William's wife. "Lady Carey, do you share your husband's views on the subject of music? I well recall your favoring a soiree at Knebworth with an excellent performance on the violin."

"Aye, Lord Lytton," she answered. "I'm the musician in the family. But if you expect me to say my husband is wrong about anything he has to say, even on a subject beyond his ken, well, you'll be sorely disappointed."

"I believe we can all applaud such loyalty in a wife," Philip said, while glancing at Marie.

"It's true, this is not my field of expertise," Sir William conceded. "I'm not a man of the arts but of science. At least, military science."

"I can vouch for your expertise in that field," Lord Burnley interjected.

Philip nodded in approval. "I have no doubt, Sir William, that you are very knowledgeable in military matters. And I am sure you would agree that the future will see many innovations and new ideas in the way wars are fought."

"Well, I don't know about that. I think if you study the career of the Great Duke, you'll learn all there is to know about tactics and strategy."

"But Wellington did not have to contend with modern innovations, such as railroads and the telegraph, that proved of such importance in our recent War Between the States," Philip contended.

"No. But without them, he won his war, didn't he?"

As the conversation continued around the table, Lytton fell into silence and began, with the sharp eye of a novelist, to assess Marie's appearance. He did not think her especially beautiful. But that didn't matter; he knew too well that beauty did not guarantee a congenial temperament. Her complexion was clear but pale, suggesting she may have recently recovered from illness. She still appeared delicate, which he found attractive. Her hair was simply and becomingly parted over a prominent forehead. Her violet blue eyes, shaded by long lashes, suggested an intelligence not evident in her superficial chatter. Disguised intellect was a quality that appealed to Lytton in a woman. He wanted to know more about her—indeed, he longed to learn her history.

The dinner conversation was drawing to a close. Men glanced surreptitiously at their watches, and women looked meaningfully at their husbands. Lytton, who had remained silent for some time, spoke up to bemoan the reams of correspondence awaiting him at his residence.

"I suppose," he said to Mark, "that, with the convening of the new Parliament approaching, you would not be free to come down to Torquay to assist me, is that so?"

"Yes, unfortunately. The new Ministry will fully occupy the time, not only of the M.P.'s, but of those of us who report on their doings." Mark knew Lytton so well that it took him only a moment to realize the real purpose of his question. "But I have an idea," he continued. "It just occurred to me, Lord Lytton, that Philip here might prove of great assistance to you. I can attest that he is a thorough man of business and is both able and energetic. You can rely on him for any task. If he is willing, I could, as it were, lend him to you to serve as your unofficial private secretary."

Philip was, of course, willing and responded with a brief speech of appreciation. Once the matter was settled, Lytton looked pleased with himself. "I know that you will do a good job and that you will enjoy Torquay." He was addressing Philip but giving his attention to Marie. "I believe," he continued, "that Torquay has the nearest thing to a southern climate to be found here in the White Isle."

"Lord Lytton," Marie responded, "it's not very often that I'm left speechless. But this is one of those times. This is truly an occasion to remember."

"Then each and all of us shall remember it together," Lytton said in an oracular tone. "The future is clear. I will pass the winter at Torquay and then repair to Knebworth to greet the coming of Spring. To do that, I shall invite each and every one at this table to share the vernal accession with us."

The promised invitation drew forth a chorus of approval from all present. "My goodness," Marie thought, "Torquay and Knebworth. Not bad. Not bad at all."

CHAPTER TWO

A WINTER AT TORQUAY

Gradually, Marie and Philip adapted to life with Lord Lytton in the resort town of Torquay. Demanding as he was with Philip, Lytton was always considerate with Marie. Still, there were many things he wanted her to do as well. Needing some time to herself, Marie formed a habit of arising before dawn to go to the edge of the cliffs that overlook the sea. It took only a matter of minutes for her to walk down the hill from Argyll House, on Warren Road, where Lytton and the Deflorettes resided, to the rocks where she could sit and gaze at the panorama before her. One morning in early March, more than two months after she and Philip had taken up residence in Torquay, she began to contemplate the events of the preceding weeks. In the morning twilight, she could see the whitecaps below as the wind whipped up the waves. She looked out at the horizon, imagining that she could see all the way across the ocean, half expecting the spires of Charleston to tower in the distance. Eventually, the sun rose before her, reminding her that she was actually looking eastward to the Channel, not westward to America. She laughed out loud at her own mistake. Am I really that homesick after all, she wondered.

She enjoyed her life in Torquay, even if it did not provide as many social opportunities as she had expected, nor as many chances for Philip to form new friendships that might enable him to advance his career. But they kept busy! Marie's tasks included organizing stacks of papers in the office, as well as sewing and mending. She truly enjoyed needlework. It fully occupied her mind while she was doing it, and the products of her exertions gave her lasting pleasure once completed. She once even knitted a pair of woolen slippers for Lytton. The latter was often ill, or, at least, purported to be, and Marie served as nurse as well as seamstress.

But Lytton proved he meant what he said when he encouraged Marie to cultivate her musical talent. He urged her to take the entrance examination at the Royal Academy of Music, pledging to pay the fees if she were admitted as a student. He advised her to practice on the piano in the lobby of the nearby Miller's Hotel, and Marie did so whenever she found the time.

On one occasion, when he was feeling unusually fit, Lytton accompanied her there, and she delighted him by playing and singing "Believe me, if all those endearing young charms," a song whose sentimental lyrics Lytton loved, in part because they had been composed by Tom Moore, who had befriended Lytton when the latter was a struggling young author.

She also enjoyed going to Miller's Hotel because it was there that she met the only new friends she made in Torquay: Mrs. Tillett, a middle-aged widow, and her spinster daughter Frances, who looked to be about 25 years old, the same age as Marie. They reminded Marie of the many gossipy ladies she knew in the Carolinas, and, although she aspired to move on from that kind of life, she could not help but like the Tilletts and enjoy their company. They were so simple and unaffected, unlike some of the people she had met in her forays into high society. Plus, the Tilletts greatly admired Marie's musical talent, which bolstered her sometimes fragile ego.

Mrs. Tillett and her daughter both described themselves as devoted readers of Lytton's books and were highly impressed that Marie knew the great novelist personally. "While I've enjoyed all his books," Mrs. Tillett remarked one day, "my favorite is the one he called My Novel."

"What about you, Frances? Do you have a favorite?"

"Oh, yes. I just loved What Will He Do with It?"

"Well, would you like to know which is his favorite?" Marie asked in a conspiratorial tone.

"Oh, yes! Tell us, please."

"It's his next one. Whatever that is."

The three ladies shared a laugh, and from then on, whenever they got together, they also shared a running joke that Lytton was then writing a book called *Whatever That Is*.

✻✻✻

In early December, when Philip began working as private secretary to Lord Lytton, he found it to be a demanding job. When he first got down to business in the little room in Argyll House that would serve as his office, Philip started going through the stack of unopened mail and messages on the desk. Some of these had been sent directly to Lytton in Torquay; others had been forwarded from either Knebworth or from Lytton's London residence in Grosvenor Square. There was a great deal of correspondence from Lytton's publishers, as well as many letters from "devoted readers" who wanted an autograph.

Near the bottom of the pile was an official-looking envelope that had been posted many weeks earlier but had remained unopened. "It's from the Office of the Home Secretary," Philip informed his employer.

Lytton shook his head wearily. "I suppose it's best you read it to me." Philip did so:

Dear Lytton,

It is vital that I meet with you here at the earliest date convenient to you. Information has come to my attention relative to certain untoward events about which you have no doubt read in the press. The matter is too sensitive to commit to paper. I know you will provide whatever assistance you can.

It is possible, with the elections upcoming, that I may not remain in office much longer. In the event of that unhappy outcome, please contact Col. Fielding of the detective department. He is able and discreet. I rely on you.

Yours truly,
Gathorne Hardy

"What do you make of that?" Philip asked. "For the then-Home Secretary to have summoned you in that way, well, it must have been a matter of importance." Lytton looked thoughtful but remained silent for what, to Philip, seemed a long time before he spoke. "I will go to London for a few days, once I feel up to it. You will remain here and look after things. There's a manuscript of my Horace in the bedroom. I was reviewing it last night before going to sleep. While I'm away, please copy it over in your fine Spencerian script. Blackwood has been complaining about difficulty in deciphering my scrawl."

While Lytton was away in London, Philip kept busy at his assigned tasks. After an absence that lasted just over a week, Lytton returned to Torquay shortly before Christmas.

"What can you tell me about the outcome of your journey?" Philip asked him breathlessly.

Lytton looked tired but answered with unusual enthusiasm. "Excellent news! On the train returning here, I chanced to encounter Lord Henry Worthing and his wife. They're going to visit us over Christmas. Isn't that splendid?"

"Splendid, indeed," Philip replied, trying without success to disguise his displeasure.

"Oh, I know he sometimes gives the wrong impression," Lytton said reassuringly. "He's really a fine fellow, even if he doesn't like Americans."

"In that case, my Lord, he definitely gave the correct impression."

"Well, regardless, he's a true classical scholar, the best one at Cambridge in his time. Placed in the top division of the first class in the Classical Tripos. Won the Browne medal two years consecutively. Bring me the manuscript, if you would, Philip."

Philip then retrieved the copy he had made of the manuscript of Lytton's latest work, a translation of The Odes and Epodes of Horace. Lytton quickly scanned the document.

"Wonderful. You've done an excellent job of transcribing it. Lord Henry will have no difficulty reading it tomorrow."

"Tomorrow?"

"Yes, he promised to come by after lunch. Unfortunately, I don't believe I will be able to receive him. My journey has exhausted me utterly. I expect to be confined to my bed for some time. I count on you and Marie to see to it that he has everything he requires."

"You can depend upon us, sir. But may I ask one question? Did your journey shed any light on the political situation?"

"It did indeed. On the return trip, Lord Henry regaled me with all the political news. He seemed very up to date about what constituencies would likely require by-elections in the coming year."

No doubt, Philip thought, Lord Henry would dearly love to make himself the candidate in one of those by-elections. But Philip adhered to the old saying: a diplomat must measure his words to disguise his thoughts. "You are fortunate, Lord Lytton, to have such good friends as will readily share, not only the news of the day but also the likely course of future events."

The next morning, as anticipated, Lytton's symptoms worsened, and a doctor was summoned. Medications were provided, which soon put the patient into a deep sleep. Thus, when Lord Henry arrived at two o'clock, it fell to Philip to explain the situation to him.

"No matter. Just bring me the manuscript and show me a comfortable place to read it." Apparently taking Philip and Marie to be servants, Lord Henry added, "And you, Missus, may bring me a glass of Madeira." Philip started to remind Lord Henry of their previous meeting, but the latter ignored him and seated himself at Philip's desk. He was at once engrossed in reading the manuscript of Lytton's translation of the poetry written by Horace in the early days of the Roman Empire. Occasionally, Lord Henry would pause to tell Marie to fetch something or other, a pillow for his chair, a reading lamp, or more wine. Otherwise, he remained silent, with an enigmatic half-smile on his face.

Having finished with as much of the manuscript as he cared to read, he stood up and, after muttering something in French, departed unceremoniously.

"Well, God bless him," Marie remarked disdainfully. "I don't know how you'll explain that to Lord Lytton. But, Philip, I know, if anyone can, you can."

"There's always a tactful way to say anything that needs saying. But I expect Lord Henry will take care of that himself."

"Well, I couldn't understand what he said right there at the end, but I could tell from his tone of voice he was being sarcastic. But tell me, what did he say and why did he say it in French?"

Philip chuckled. "He said it in French because he was paraphrasing a famous remark by a French general during the Crimean War. What Lord Henry said translates to: 'It is magnificent, but it is not Horace.'"

"That sounds like him, all right. I tell you, either he is very rich or that pretty wife of his is some kind of saint."

The following day, Lytton received a note from Lord Henry, delivered by special messenger. The note read: "Thank you for giving me the opportunity of perusing your Horace. It has that literary quality for which you are so well known. I am sure it will receive all the attention it merits."

The fact that Lytton was under doctor's orders gave Marie a good deal more free time than she had had before. Indeed, when the doctor returned to look in on Lytton, Marie took the opportunity to stroll over to Miller's Hotel to play the piano, hoping also to find the Tilletts in the lobby. Marie played a selection from Chopin's "Revolutionary Etude," then scanned the lobby to see if her friends happened to be there. They were not, but she did hear the sound of someone clapping nearby.

"Monty Kelly," she shouted, recognizing a friend from home. "I almost didn't recognize you behind those red whiskers," she added as she gave him a friendly embrace.

"It's been a few years, Marie, but you still play as beautifully as ever. I'm so glad to see you, though I'm surprised to find you still in England."

"I could say the same to you. What are you doing here?"

"I was a Lieutenant aboard the C.S.S. Alabama. When our dear old ship was sunk off the coast of France, I was lucky enough to be rescued and taken to England. And here I've remained ever since."

"That was lucky indeed!"

"And so, what about you, old girl? And my dear old college chum, Philip?"

"Well, it's sort of a secret, but I trust it's safe with you. Philip's an unofficial private secretary to Lord Lytton."

"Lord Lytton? You mean Bulwer Lytton, the novel writer? Faith alive, I always knew our Philip would one day rise to the top. Am I right in supposing this private secretaryship will prove a stepping stone to high office?"

"I pray for that every day. But I don't know. This country is kind of like an exclusive private club. You practically have to be born into it."

"Of that you're oh so right, indeed you are that. I don't imagine it opens any doors around here that Philip stood at the very top of the class at our dear old University of North Carolina. In these parts, unless you hold a degree from the Oxford or the Cambridge, they take you for a dunce, indeed they do."

Marie nodded vigorously. "So true. And yet I've met some dunces who have gone to those universities. But, Monty, you haven't yet told me why you've remained in this country. After all, the war has been over for three years and more."

"That's a story, I fear, I have not time to tell at the moment. But I'll break it down to two reasons. For one thing, I served on the Alabama. Oh, I know General Lee is now a college president, and his generals are safe and sound. But I do believe that while the Yankees might forgive someone who merely whipped them in battle, they'll never absolve anyone who sank millions of dollars' worth of goods they had for sale."

"You have a point," Marie agreed. "What's the other reason?"

"I'm sure that, during the war, you many times prayed for peace. I did the same myself, indeed I did. But once peace came, I found myself missing something, missing, I don't know, maybe the excitement, or the sense of purpose. Anyway, I knew I could never go back to my father's dry goods store in Wilmington."

"I suppose not. But what will you do?"

"Just what I am doing, my dear. For want of a better word, you could say I'm a soldier of fortune."

"But just what does that mean, in practical terms?"

"Well, here, dear Marie, I must borrow your very own words: it's sort of a secret. But, in this case, it's a secret that would be best not to share even with you. I do hope, when next I come this way, I can dine with you and Philip and have a good, long talk about all that goes on in this world that seems never without a need for soldiers of one kind or another."

"I look forward to that with all my heart. But, please, good old Monty, take care of yourself. It's a dangerous world out there."

"'Tis indeed, my lovely, dangerous for one and all. So, now, you be pleased to remember to take care of yourself as well."

As the weeks went by, Marie thought often about that chance meeting with Monty Kelly. She told Philip about it, and even he was mystified. As dawn turned to daylight that morning in March, Marie wondered whether her encounter with the "soldier of fortune" had been but a dream.

When she got back to Argyll House, she found Philip had already finished breakfast and was busy writing at his desk.

"What has he got you doing today, writing the first draft of his next novel?" she asked.

"Hardly. But the news is that our stay at Torquay will soon be coming to a close."

"Really? Then I suppose his new book will be called, What Will I Do Without Them?"

"Not at all. We'll still be with him. Right now, I'm making a guest list for the so-called reunion he's planning to host at Knebworth. Remember, at Lord Burnley's dinner, he promised to invite all present to Knebworth at the beginning of April?"

"I shall never forget it."

"That's why I'm making a list of all the people who were at that dinner, as well as some of Lytton's Hertfordshire neighbors, a term I use loosely, by the way. I am looking up the addresses in this address book of his, so he'll have everything he needs to write the invitations. Fortunately, he'll take care of that part himself."

"What about us?"

"Oh, we're invited too, of course. Here's the plan. He's leaving on Monday, first to take care of some business in London and then to open up Knebworth. We'll look after things here until the 28th and then take the train to Hertfordshire. We get off at Stevenage, and he's promised we'll be met there and taken to Knebworth."

"Wonderful. I'm glad we'll have some time to get ready. It will also give me a chance to say goodbye to the Tilletts."

"Not to tell them goodbye, my dear, just au revoir."

A few days later, all the invitations had been mailed, and Lytton was off to London, leaving Philip and Marie in Torquay for the time being. With no work to do, Marie slept later than usual. Around ten, she strolled over to the hotel, leaving Philip alone at Argyll House.

With his secretarial work finished for the day, Philip looked for something to read. Lytton's bookshelves contained many volumes, covering a wide variety of subjects. Philip felt that his knowledge of the history of England was deficient, so he looked for a book on that topic. Finally, he pulled from the shelf volume 2 of Lord Stanhope's biography of William Pitt.

He read for nearly an hour before putting the book down. The story of Pitt's life caused him to reflect on his own career. He thought, Pitt became Prime Minister of England when he was only 24 years old; I'm now 28, and what have I accomplished? He had grown up thinking of himself as a North Carolinian. He had been a loyal citizen of the Confederate States of America, a nation that no longer existed. He did not find it easy to think of himself as an American. He wondered if he could make a real career for himself in England. Could he become a British subject? Could he even take part in British politics? Perhaps, the idea was not so far-fetched. Judah Benjamin, who had been a member of the Confederate cabinet, was now one of the leading barristers in London. Philip thought, Why could I not do something of the sort myself? There will be a general election here before the end of 1875. With Mark's help and Lord Lytton's influence, Philip could foresee himself being selected as a candidate. He even began to imagine what he might say in his maiden address to the House of Commons. "Mr. Speaker, I have taken a rather circuitous route to this place …."

Philip's reverie was interrupted by a knock on the door. Upon opening it, Philip immediately recognized the special messenger who had come several times before.

"Do you have another letter for Lord Lytton?"

"No, sir," the messenger said, pausing to reread the name on the envelope. "This one's for a, um, Mr. Deef-low-retty."

"That's close enough," said Philip smiling. "I'll take it."

He sat at his desk and opened the envelope. It contained a single piece of paper, part of a page torn from a magazine or literary journal. On one side of the paper, there were printed a few lines of a poem. On the other side, which apparently had been left blank by the publisher, someone had written in large block letters:

"DEFLORETTES: YOU MUST LEAVE ENGLAND BEFORE THE END OF EASTER OR DIE. THIS IS YOUR ONLY WARNING."

Philip stared at the words for several minutes. Finally, he placed the paper back in its envelope, which he then put into his jacket pocket. His thoughts turned to Marie, who no doubt was at that very moment happily singing a beautiful aria to the delight of all lucky enough to be in the lobby of Miller's hotel.

CHAPTER THREE

INVITATIONS TO KNEBWORTH

The Dionysus Club in London was unique: a gentleman's club instituted for no purpose other than to offer its members the finer things of life. It boasted the most appealing menu and the most esteemed wine cellar anywhere in Mayfair. For Lord Burnley, it was a home away from home.

Although he employed an excellent cook at Rockbridge House, Burnley, a bachelor, seldom dined there unless he had guests. The prospect of dining alone depressed him. Consequently, he earned a reputation for being the most "clubbable" man in London. As Lord Henry Worthing put it: "Burnley scribbles articles on ornithology in order to join the Athenaeum; he keeps up with literature to fit in at the Rambler; he dabbles in politics in order that he might dine at the Carlton Club; and he frequents the Dionysus because their claret helps him forget birds, books, and bootlicking."

One evening in March, Burnley dined at the Dionysus with Mark Hornell as his guest. The two friends were strikingly unalike in manner: Mark, always alert, was quick to enthuse about the latest developments in the world of politics and politicians, being equally delighted to expound on those he deplored as on those he extolled. Burnley, on the other hand, was as grave in manner as he was gray in appearance. As Mark recounted the latest follies of the Gladstone ministry, Burnley responded with reminiscences of his own service in the War Office, many years earlier. As the evening wore on, the two friends focused on finishing their bottle of Chateau Margaux '58. Before they had done so, a waiter approached Lord Burnley and handed him a letter: "This was just delivered by special messenger, milord." Burnley nodded and opened the envelope. "It's something that will interest you, Mark. It's from Lytton."

"Oh yes, I've been expecting to hear from him myself. Remember the reunion at Knebworth he promised that evening at Rockbridge?"

"I certainly do. And, yes, it is indeed an invitation to stay at Knebworth during Easter Week." Burnley frowned as he finished reading the letter.

"Mark, this next part is so singular I must read it aloud." Burnley then read a portion of the letter in a mock theatrical voice: "'It will be not only an occasion to renew old friendships, but to celebrate a new friendship with a young couple I had the good fortune to encounter at your very own table. I have always believed that, when young, one should seek the company of those who are older; and, when old, the company of those who are younger.' My word!"

"Well," Mark responded, "they do say Lytton never wrote even an invitation to dinner without an eye to posterity. But I am glad to know he's gotten along so well with the Deflorettes."

"You should not be surprised. Remember how taken he was with them at my dinner party? If I recall correctly, that young fellow from South America used to work for you, didn't he, Mark?"

"He did indeed and may again. But he was not from South America, but from the American South."

Burnley ignored the correction. "And that wife of his, quite a flirt, wasn't she, Mark? I've never trusted women like that. I suppose she has Lytton wrapped around her little finger. She must be up to something."

"Well, if she is, we'll no doubt find out about it in April at Knebworth. That is, assuming a similar letter is on its way to summon Mrs. Hornell and me, and assuming that you decide to accept the invitation. I have the impression you're doubtful about doing so."

"On the contrary," Burnley replied. "I wouldn't miss this for the world."

✯✯✯

Sir William Carey shifted slightly in his easy chair, the better to catch the afternoon sunlight, as he read the sixth and last volume of Thomas Carlyle's biography of Frederick the Great that had recently been published. Sir William was so engrossed in the book that he was hardly aware of the presence of his wife, Cora, who was on the sofa across the room and busy with her knitting. With the sound of a knock, she sprang to her feet.

Sir William, without looking up from his book, barked: "The door!"

"Aye, I thought it might be the door," Cora answered. Despite her girth, she was quick on her feet and had already gotten to the entrance hall. "It must be Miss Hickman. I had invited her to tea."

Sir William continued to read. After several minutes, he looked about. "Where is she, Cora?"

"You mean Miss Hickman? It was not she at the door but rather the afternoon post."

"Anything of interest?"

"Aye. We got three invitations, no less. Care to read them?"

"No. Just tell me where we're invited and by whom."

"As you wish, m'dear. The first is an invitation to dinner from Mrs. Dexter."

"Who on earth is Mrs. Dexter?"

"I think you've met her. She lives right here in Watford. Husband manages one of the mills."

"Oh, a social climber. I've no time for that."

Lady Carey smiled. She did not much care for Mrs. Dexter. "Very well, we go on to the second one, which I expect will prove more pleasing to you. It's for a dinner commemorating the statue of the late Lord Herbert that was erected in front of the War Office."

But Sir William's expression made clear that he was not pleased. "What Sidney Herbert knew about running a war could fit into that thimble on your finger, with space left over. Imagine a war with a woman being the only true hero to come out of it!"

"Oh, you mean Miss Nightingale. But, my dear, I'm sure you'll agree, had it not been for the support Lord Herbert provided as War Secretary, no one would ever have heard of Florence Nightingale, and that would have gone hard with our soldiers in Crimea. Oh, by the way, I see her name listed here as one of those who will speak at the dinner."

Sir William shrugged his shoulders. "I suppose I should not speak ill about the dead."

"You needn't make up your mind for now," Lady Carey continued. "The dinner's not 'til May. So, let's move on to the third, which I expect you'll like even less. It's from Lord Lytton, inviting us to Knebworth House during Easter week."

The Careys had just begun to discuss Lytton's letter when there was another knock on the door. This time it was Miss Hickman come to tea. She was a small, gray-haired lady in her seventies who looked very frail as she walked slowly toward the tea table, all the while peering through wire-rimmed glasses at the floor in front of her, as if she feared tripping over something. Once seated, however, her apparent frailty vanished, as she spoke with a strong voice and a quiet confidence that invested even casual remarks with an aura of profundity. Miss Hickman's genuine excellence as a conversationalist derived, not so much from what she had to say, but from the intensity with which she listened to others, without ever interrupting them.

Cora greeted her elderly friend warmly and began the discussion as she poured the tea. "Just when you arrived, Miss Hickman, William and I were discussing an invitation from Lord Lytton to spend a few days at Knebworth House, along with some mutual friends. We're debating whether we should accept or not."

Miss Hickman considered the matter for a few moments. "I was wondering," she began, "as to what might be the reason for your hesitation. Nowadays, most people would jump at the chance to spend some time with a famous man at a famous house. I believe, by the way, that it would be a near run thing as to whether

Lord Lytton or Charles Dickens would rank as the most popular novelist of our day. Besides that, Lytton is a man not without political influence. Aside from Sir Stafford Northcote, I can think of no one else who is on such friendly terms with both Mr. Gladstone and Mr. Disraeli."

"We know all that, of course," said Sir William rather impatiently. "And we've been to Knebworth before. The reason for my hesitating is that Lytton's idea of entertaining his guests is to expose them to a lot of mumbo jumbo and poppycock: you know, fortune telling, or communicating with the dead, and all that sort of thing."

"And then there's that young American couple," Cora added.

"Oh, that's right," Sir William said, "I had forgotten about them."

"I think I understand," Miss Hickman said as she leaned her head back and looked upward as she pondered the matter. After a few minutes of thought, she gave her opinion. "I appreciate your discomfort with spiritualism, Sir William. But, I have heard that the practice of conducting seances has become very widespread in America. I expect this is a consequence of the untimely deaths of so many young men in their recent Civil War. No doubt the bereaved derive some comfort from the hope of communicating with the loved and lost."

"Deaths are only to be expected in war," Sir William responded coldly, "and all that's 'derived' is the money that a bunch of charlatans derive out of the pockets of those gullible enough to believe in them."

"You are certainly correct, Sir William. One should assume any so-called medium is pretending to be something he or she is not, unless proven otherwise. Lord Lytton, I'm sure, knows that as well. But don't you suppose he indulges in such experiments for no reason other than that he enjoys them? After all, if you go to a performance of Hamlet, you don't complain afterward that Macready is not really a Danish prince."

"My husband would be the one person to make such a complaint," Cora said with a laugh. "But I think I gave you the wrong impression about the American couple. They're not mediums. Each is a kind of protege to Lord Lytton."

"How did two young Americans become proteges of a preeminent English novelist? That would seem a most unlikely turn of events."

"Unlikely? It's incredible, but quite true nonetheless," Sir William said somewhat ruefully. "Now, I don't know all the facts; I've only encountered those people a couple of times. All I know is the young man came to this country as some sort of agent for the Southern Confederacy and joined up with a nest of fellow traitors. After they lost their war, he remained in this country, no doubt to make more mischief."

"I see. He had been representing the southern states of America, and now he's stranded here and living by his wits."

"That's about it, Miss Hickman," Cora said, "and I want you to know I don't believe he's as treacherous as William seems to think. I had been seated next to the young man—he was verra good looking—at a dinner at Rockbridge House last year." Here, Cora interrupted herself by laughing loudly. "The thing was," she explained, "he spoke with one of those accents the like of which I had never heard before excepting on the stage. As he talked, I couldn't help but burst into laughter. I know it was rude, and I was truly ashamed of myself, but I could hardly understand what he was saying. I must say he was very kind about it and seemed to take no notice."

"Interesting. And what about the young lady? His wife, I assume. How did she impress you?"

"I had no trouble understanding her," Sir William said firmly. "She claimed to be a musical genius and soon had Lytton believing it. Lytton then made the young man his secretary, all the while hoping to make the girl, um, that is to say, to add the girl to his circle of friends."

"You made your meaning very clear, Sir William," said Miss Hickman, "even if you intended to obscure it. Given what we might call the state of affairs at Knebworth, I am surprised that you are not more anxious to attend the proceedings, out of curiosity if nothing more."

"You have persuaded me, Miss Hickman. Cora, let us accept Lord Lytton's kind invitation, post-haste."

Cora smiled. "I'd best get back into practice on the violin."

✲✲✲

Lady Henry Worthing (Daphne to her friends; Daffy to her close friends) had come to dread the arrival of the post. So much of it came from merchants demanding the settlement of overdue accounts. While both Lord Henry, the younger son of a Marquess, and Lady Henry, the daughter of a banker in the City of London, came from wealthy families, their own incomes fell short of the cost of their posh lifestyle. Their sole concession to economy was their residence in a flat in Mecklenburgh Square in the Bloomsbury section of London, where rent was considerably less than in Mayfair or Belgravia. The location had the added advantage of being within walking distance of University College, London, and the British Museum, places where Lord Henry might research the books that he hoped would bring him fame and fortune, books that as yet remained unwritten.

Daphne was delighted one day to find amid the dunning notices an invitation from Lord Lytton to spend a few days at Knebworth House. But she was dismayed when her husband seemed disinclined to go.

"Just give me one good reason why we should offend Lord Lytton by refusing his kind invitation," she said.

"He would not be offended, my dear, he would be relieved. After all, his reason for calling for this convocation is to exhibit the 'brilliance' of that Yankee whippersnapper he made his private secretary. My presence would certainly defeat that purpose."

"Excuse me for contradicting you, Henry, but I must point out that the young man you reference is not a Yankee. He had formerly been a representative of the southern American states, the ones who fought against the Yankees. And, while I agree that the gathering would largely consist of persons who are not your intellectual equals, is that a reason to avoid it?"

"Certainly not; for if it were, I should never leave the house. But there's another argument for opposing the motion. Don't you recall that silly little wife of his? What a chatterbox! You were so lucky that night at Burnley's that you had my lanky frame between yourself and that fountain of babble."

Daphne remained silent for a moment, then walked over to the window overlooking the beautiful garden that lay in the center of the square. She then chose her words carefully, enunciating each one with precision.

"I hate to bring up some practical points, Henry, but you leave me little choice. You say you have political ambitions. You want to be in Parliament. But to be a politician, you must be politic. Of course, you're a superior person, but must you always remind everyone of it? Don't you think it's time you learned to accept people for what they are?"

For several minutes, Daphne stood before the window in silence, gazing at the street below. A mounted policeman was riding around the square. The rhythmic sound made by his horse's hooves had a calming effect. Lord Henry stepped toward his wife and embraced her; she smiled as he whispered in her ear, "Daffy, would you mind sending Lytton our acceptance? I don't have time to write a short letter."

CHAPTER FOUR

A DAY IN THE LIFE
OF A FAMOUS NOVELIST

Angus Jackson, Lord Lytton's butler and general factotum, was relaxing over a cup of tea in the servants' hall at Lytton's London residence on Grosvenor Square, when the cook, obviously in a state of anxiety, approached him.

"I am so very sorry, Mr. Jackson, I seem to 'ave overslept a bit this morning. Oh, my, it's already 8:30! Is 'is Lordship awaiting breakfast?"

"Calm down, Mrs. Roberts. Everything's all right. Last night, as usual, I placed seven cigars on his Lordship's night table. When I looked in on him this morning at eight o'clock, I found he had smoked all seven before going to sleep. So, I'm letting him sleep on until nine."

"Oh, that's very good news, thank you, Mr. Jackson." Mrs. Roberts settled down on a chair and breathed a sigh of relief. She was fifty-three years of age but looked older. Her voice was hoarse—overstrained by years of yelling at lackadaisical kitchen maids—but she tried to affect a certain gentility in her speech that imperfectly disguised her Cockney origins. She had served as a cook for decades but had worked for Lord Lytton less than a year. She was accordingly very deferential to Jackson.

"Never fear, Mr. Jackson. There will be no repetition of my tardiness this morning. And you can rest assured I'll have a fine breakfast ready for 'is Lordship when 'e comes down."

And true to her words, Mrs. Roberts had a full English breakfast ready when, about an hour later, Lytton came to the table. He looked dour and distracted and ate very little of the food Mrs. Roberts had prepared for him. He drank one sip of tea and then poured the rest into a glass, which he then took to his study. There, he reviewed the notes he had made the previous night.

At eleven o'clock, Jackson went to the study to deliver a missive just received from a special messenger, as well as the morning post, which, to Lytton's delight, included a letter from Marie. Jackson found his employer now in a much better mood than before. Lytton smiled broadly when the butler asked him if there was anything else he needed.

"I need a better memory, Jackson. I'm sure I had an appointment of some kind this afternoon, but for the life of me, I cannot remember what it was about. Can you enlighten me?"

"Indeed, my Lord. Colonel Fielding is coming here at two o'clock. And a messenger just brought this letter from the Colonel a few minutes ago."

Lytton's eyes widened as he scanned the message. "Not only is Colonel Fielding coming here, but he's also bringing Mr. Henry Bruce with him. Things must be in a sorry state indeed if the new Home Secretary finds it necessary to pay me a visit."

"No doubt Mr. Bruce recognizes that he would profit from drawing on your long experience in matters of state. Should I have sherry on hand to offer the gentlemen when they arrive?"

"I think not, Jackson. Mr. Bruce plans to amend the licensing laws to restrict the hours of drink. Out of respect for our thirsty fellow countrymen, we should offer their bête noire nothing but tea."

"Very good, my Lord."

"Now, I must put the problems of the Home Office out of mind and concentrate on my own work."

But once Jackson had left the study, Lytton did not immediately get to work. Instead, like a schoolboy reading the sports pages before doing his homework, Lytton eagerly read and reread Marie's short note.

Then, with a sigh, Lytton turned his attention to drafting the new novel. Time and again, he would write paragraphs, then cross them out, and start again. Nonetheless, the story he wished to tell was gradually becoming clearer in his mind. This book would differ radically from anything he had written before.

Lytton wanted to demonstrate the futility of the ideas of the utopian reformers of the day by showing that, if they should succeed in putting their theories into practice, the results would be disastrous. These so-called idealists sought to create a world where there would be no distinction between the classes, no distinction between the sexes, indeed, no distinction of any kind. No one would be rich, and no one would be poor. No one would strive to better himself. Everyone would have just as much as he required, but nothing more. If all that came to pass, what kind of world would result?

To Lytton, the prospect was repellent. He believed that life in a world of absolute equality would not be worth living. Without the freedom to be different, there would be no excellence; without excellence, there would be no achievement; without achievement, there would be no creativity; and without creativity, there would be no art. In short, a world of deadly uniformity would be too boring to bear.

Even the goal of perpetual peace might be achieved only at too high a price. Lytton, while not a scientist, understood that there were forces in nature not yet harnessed by mankind. He suspected that electrical energy, in some form yet to be discovered, might be one of these forces. He had speculated about such forces in his occult writings. Might it not be possible for scientists someday to discover how to unleash these as yet little-understood forces, and thereby create weapons infinitely more destructive than any yet imagined? Perhaps, he thought, such weapons could launch attacks over a distance of hundreds of miles with such devastating effect as to reduce a city the size of London to ashes in a matter of minutes. Thus, the perpetual peace dreamed of by philosophers would be achieved because the consequences of war would be too horrifying to contemplate, and mankind would be doomed forever to contemplate such horrors.

To construct the story he had in mind, Lytton needed a central character who, coming from the world as it is, would discover the world that is to come. He hit on the idea that the character should be an American. After all, America itself was a kind of New World, lacking both the traditions and inhibitions of the Old World. An American would therefore be best suited to assess the strengths as well as the defects of this imagined world of the future. It occurred to Lytton that Philip might make an excellent model for the hero of the story. Philip had the tact and diplomatic skill one would need to make his way in a world so different from the one he had previously known. Wasn't that what Philip had been doing since his arrival in England?

Might not Marie likewise be a model for a character in the new book? The idea appealed to Lytton; Marie was often on his mind. He really believed she possessed a kind of musical genius and feared that her self-deprecatory attitude about her talent would limit her achievement. Once, back in Torquay, when he raised the subject with her, she went so far as to respond, "I sometimes doubt, especially of late, if I am even fond of music myself."

He then scolded her. "Marie, it is impossible that you should not be. Genius can never be untrue to itself and must love that in which it excels and attains to glory." Yet, despite his scolding, Lytton found Marie's modesty quite appealing.

Lytton saw in Marie the embodiment of a feminine ideal, combining both gentleness and strength. Her hands looked very small and delicate and yet were so nimble and even forceful when she played the piano. She denied that she had any special talent and yet always carried herself with a dignity that left no doubt of her pride in her own identity.

Yes, Lytton thought, I must someday create a character based on dear Marie. But it cannot be a character in the book now contemplated. All the women in this book must be of the Amazonian variety, representing the utopian vision of the equality of the sexes. The portrait he would pen of Marie must await a later novel.

Literary work had to be set aside at two o'clock. The meeting with Mr. Secretary Bruce and Colonel Fielding then began and lasted more than an hour. Once his distinguished visitors had left, Lytton sadly told Jackson, "It appears I will have to remain in town a few days longer than originally planned. Pray make the necessary arrangements. I will go presently to my study to write to Mr. Deflorette about the change in plans. It should take me no more than a quarter hour. The letter must then be posted immediately."

But Lytton did not address the letter to Philip, but rather to Marie, in part because he wanted to respond to the correspondence she had written to him. His letter began by acknowledging hers that he had read earlier that day.

Dear Marie,

I got your pretty little note this morning. Your kind words cheered me in a moment of depression. I was much struck with your graceful and poetic image of harmony as an essential to the life of the musical artist. You can expect me to "borrow" your words in some future book. You provided a touching picture of a young woman's heart and her longings. I hope to create a literary portrait of a woman of genius, if I am granted sufficient time and energy to complete such a task.

Meanwhile, the current book advances slowly. But I now have a plan in mind. If I fully realize what I envision, it will floor all my literary foes. I realize that it will find readers only if it is published as an anonymous work, which will excite curiosity and puzzle people.

By the way, I dined with Disraeli on Saturday. He had gotten together some of the handsomest ladies in town, the Duchess of Sutherland and Lady Hamilton, among others. But they did not make me forget the charming face of my absent correspondent.

Please tell Philip some unexpected business will require me to remain in town several days longer than originally planned, and he should therefore postpone the trip to Knebworth until Easter Monday. Remember to take the train to Stevenage station. You will be met there and transported to Knebworth. Have Philip send me a note stating the expected arrival time. Meanwhile, you will have the opportunity to enjoy the pleasures of Torquay a little longer than expected. Yours, L.

CHAPTER FIVE

THE LAST DAYS OF TORQUAY

Marie was stunned by Philip's angry reaction to Lytton's letter. It was so unlike him that she stared in disbelief at her usually placid, self-controlled husband. Nor would he offer any explanation for his being so upset. But he insisted they should not go to Knebworth at any time.

"But Lord Lytton has sent out the invitations," Marie reminded him, "and he told his friends we will be there. Besides, he is your employer, and so is Mark, who was also invited. You cannot refuse them. Philip, you're just not making sense."

"I am making sense, because we should leave this country and go home as soon as it can be arranged."

"But why?"

"For all the reasons we've discussed so many times. This is not our country. The English have ways of doing things that we do not understand. Here, everything must be explained to us. Back home, nothing need be explained to us. The Carolinas are home. Here, we are strangers in a strange land."

"I do not believe that, Philip, and until now, neither did you. So many people have been so very kind to us and have helped us in so many ways. Don't you remember what it was like for us when the Confederacy began to crumble? We were left with nothing. Remember what it was like to be hungry? And how sick I got?"

"I do remember. I was so afraid I would lose you. That's why I want to take you away from here now, Marie. This country might kill you if we stay. The climate, I mean, it's so cold and damp. The warm Carolina sun would work wonders for you. You're not entirely recovered even now."

"I know, but I would rather die than let down the people who have been so good to us. Especially Mark, who provided us a livelihood, and, of course, Lord Lytton, who readily took us under his wing."

"I know, I know." Philip was beginning to weaken. He could not tell Marie about the threatening letter. How could he make her understand? "Listen," he said in a softer tone than before. "I'm also trying to be practical. There are things I want to accomplish in this world. But I'll never amount to anything in

England. I went to the University of North Carolina, not Cambridge or Oxford. I have friends and family in Carolina. I can make a career there. Perhaps a political career. Marie, the war has been over some four years. It's time we went home."

"Philip, I just can't wrap my mind around this sudden decision. I don't see why a short delay in our going to Knebworth should have put you, of all people, in a panic and made you change your mind about everything. But, dear Philip, please understand. I know the duties of a wife. Whither thou goest, I will go; and where thou lodgest, I will lodge; thy political party will be my political party. But, seriously, on Easter Monday, whither thou goest will be to Knebworth House! While we're there, you can discuss all your plans with Lord Lytton, and if you still want to go home, then we'll go home. A week or so cannot make any difference."

Philip gave way, but his mood did not improve. The next morning, Marie was relieved to get out of Argyll House to take her usual walk down to the cliffs overlooking the sea. This time, however, the beautiful view failed to cheer her. She did not stay long. She made her way to Brown's Hotel, hoping and praying the Tilletts would be there.

To Marie's delight, she found her friends at their usual table, and they seemed equally pleased to see her.

"I was much afraid I might never see you again," Mrs. Tillett said. "You see, Frances and I will be leaving Torquay tomorrow."

"Oh, I didn't realize you'd be leaving so soon."

"Well, Marie, the winter is over, isn't it? And that ends the Torquay season. Frances and I always return home in time for Easter services at St. John's Church. That's the church nearest our home, you see."

"Home," Marie repeated with emphasis. "There seems to be something mystical about that word. But, anyway, where is home for you?"

"We live in Hitchin," Frances answered. "It's a lovely town in Hertfordshire."

"Hertfordshire!" Marie shouted. "Why, that's where Knebworth is—Lord Lytton's home. Y'all are his neighbors!"

The Tilletts both laughed at that remark. "Oh no, my dear," said Mrs. Tillett, "we might reside in the same county, but we live in different worlds. I have never been near the place, but I have seen pictures of Knebworth. Why, it's practically a palace, isn't it? Hitchin, on the other hand, is just a typical English village, populated by ordinary folks like us."

"I'm afraid," Frances interjected, "Mother may not be giving you a complete picture of our town. Hitchin is actually a rather important place. In point of fact, Cambridge University has selected Hitchin to be the site of its first college for women."

"Oh, I know that," said Mrs. Tillett, slightly annoyed. "But I fail to see what possible use a university education could be for a woman."

"If I were a few years younger," responded Frances with unusual firmness, "I should like to attend this new college."

Marie sensed that she might have inadvertently triggered a quarrel between the Tilletts and, using the methods she had learned from observing Philip over the years, intervened to change the subject.

"What you say about the addition to Cambridge University is quite interesting," she began. "Lord Lytton himself is a graduate of one of the colleges at Cambridge. I have heard him speak of it several times, but my goodness, I just can't seem to remember the name of the college. Speaking of Lord Lytton, I have a question for you, Mrs. Tillett. I know that you and he don't travel in the same social circles, but I wondered, since you do live in the same county and all, have you ever seen him out and about, anywhere, maybe at a livery stable, or something of the sort?"

The question had the desired effect of getting the Tilletts laughing once again. "Unfortunately," said Mrs. Tillett, "I have never laid eyes on the man. I wish I had."

"But Father did," said Frances eagerly. "He just loved to tell the story. He told it to me several times."

"Yes, your father did like to tell good stories, and they got better with each telling. As you might suppose, Marie, my late husband was a voter in the county. There was a certain occasion—it must be about ten years ago now—he remembered seeing Lord Lytton—or I should say Sir Edward as he was then—at the hustings in Hertford. And that's what happened."

"Oh, no, Mother," Frances cut in, "there was a lot more to the story than that. Let me tell it."

"I am quite sure that Marie, such a well-brought-up young lady, is not interested in sordid stories about politics," said Mrs. Tillett, pronouncing the word "politics" as if it were a synonym for filth.

"Normally, I would agree with you, Mrs. Tillett, and thank you for the compliment, especially as it's really a compliment to my late mother. But my husband tells me he's interested in going into politics. To be a good wife for a man in politics, I had better learn as much as I can about the nasty subject."

"Let me tell it," Frances repeated eagerly.

Her mother shook her head. "If the story must be told, I will tell it. As I mentioned, it happened at the hustings about ten years ago. Sir Edward Lytton was then the Member of Parliament representing Hertfordshire. He received an appointment to the Cabinet as Colonial Secretary. So, he returned to Hertford to stand for reelection."

"Excuse me, Mrs. Tillett, I don't understand. If he was already in Parliament, why did he have to run in a special election?"

"That is the way it's done in this country. If a Member of the House of Commons wishes to accept an appointment to office, he must first be reelected by his constituency. That is the way we do it because that is the way it has always been done."

"Thank you, Mrs. Tillett. I needed to have that explained. I understand now."

"Then, to continue. Well, the election was really just a formality, wasn't it? No other candidate stood in opposition to Sir Edward. Naturally enough, he began to make his speech, giving thanks for his election."

Here, Mrs. Tillett paused, apparently trying to find the right words to describe what happened next.

"At this point, a woman in the crowd started shouting at him, hurling insults, saying he ought not be in charge of our colonies, but should be transported to one of them as a punishment for his crimes. Sir Edward asked the woman to identify herself, perhaps hoping to calm her down and win her over. Well, that wasn't going to happen. It turned out the woman was none other than his own wife!"

"She had grown so fat he didn't even recognize her!" Frances interjected.

"Well, I don't know about that. As I understand it, they had separated after some terrible quarrels, and he hadn't seen Lady Lytton in about twenty years."

"My goodness," Marie gasped, "I didn't even realize he had a wife."

"I'm sure he never speaks of her, nor would any of his friends in his presence. But to continue the story: As George—my late husband—told it, well, George said that once Sir Edward realized who the woman was, well, he simply collapsed. George thought he was stricken with a fit of apoplexy and was half expecting to read of Sir Edward's death in the papers the next morning. Some men assisted Sir Edward into a carriage and took him away somewhere. But after he had left, Lady Lytton proclaimed that, as all these people had gathered there to hear a speech, they should hear a speech. And she would be the one in the family who would make it."

"It was just awful," said Frances in a tone intended to show sympathy for Marie, who was beginning to look quite pale.

"It was indeed," Mrs. Tillett agreed. "I know how fond you are of Lord Lytton, so I will not upset you with an account of the dreadful things his wife said about him that day. She talked on and on, accusing him of every sin one can imagine, and some one can't even imagine. She absolutely transfixed the people at the hustings. It was like nothing they had ever heard before. George said the crowd listened dumbstruck to all she had to say. Even when she accused her husband of murdering their daughter years ago, the men of Herts continued to listen. They even gave her a cheer when she finally finished."

"She must be mad," Marie managed to say as she choked up. This remark unexpectedly brought smiles to the faces of the Tilletts.

"Excuse me for smiling," Mrs. Tillett said rather sheepishly, "but you'll understand when I tell you what happened next. Once Sir Edward had recovered from his shock, he had Lady Lytton committed to an insane asylum, and there she remained for I don't know how long. There was quite a hue and cry about it, and eventually she was released. According to what I heard, the alienists determined that she was perfectly sane when they talked to her about any subject other than her husband; but let anyone just mention Sir Edward, and she'd turn mad as a hatter."

"It must be a terrible thing when love turns to hate," Frances observed.

"I reckon that's true. One passion can turn into the other and be just as intense," Marie said as she daubed her face with her handkerchief.

"I'm sorry, Frances and I have upset you, especially on what may be our last meeting for a very long time."

"It's quite all right, Mrs. Tillett. I'm glad you told me. I have often wondered why Lord Lytton often looks so sad despite all his fame and fortune. Now I understand."

The Tilletts tried to raise Marie's spirits by imploring her to perform once more on the piano and perhaps sing a song. But Marie was not up to it at the moment. "Let's relax a bit and order some more tea."

"An excellent suggestion. It will do you good," said Mrs. Tillett as she beckoned a waiter to the table.

"Besides," said Marie, "I remember there was something I had meant to ask you both that I had nearly forgotten, I'm such a dunce. Just before last Christmas, I was here and happened, by chance, to meet an old friend from back in North Carolina. I haven't seen him since. I just wondered if either of you has seen him here at the hotel. He's a very distinctive looking gentleman, tall, about six feet high, well built, good looking, with dark reddish hair, and a very bushy full red beard."

The Tilletts remained silent for a moment. Mrs. Tillett shook her head. But Frances said, "I'm not sure if it's your friend, but I do remember seeing a man with such a beard. He was seated here in the lobby at a table with two other men. From where I was sitting, I was looking right at them. Mother, you probably wouldn't have noticed them because they were behind you. There was a tall man with a red beard; one of the other men was younger looking, also tall, but much thinner than the bearded man; and the third man looked older and rather stocky. Does that describe any of your friends, Marie?"

"I don't know. But you are very observant, Frances. I wish I had that trait, but I don't."

"I think I do remember the men you mean, Frances," said Mrs. Tillett. "I did catch a glimpse of them when I turned to summon a waiter. It was about a month ago they were here, wasn't it? But I don't think they were Americans. They didn't sound at all like you, Marie. From their voices, I think they were Irish."

"What were they saying?" Marie asked.

"Well, I wasn't listening now, was I? But I did happen to hear one of them mentioning something about something that was to happen in Hertfordshire. Now, it's natural enough to take notice when you're far away from home and hear something about the county where you live, don't you agree?"

"Oh, absolutely, I agree," said Marie. "And have you seen anything of any of them since then?"

"Neither hide nor wild red hair," answered Frances with a laugh.

They drank their tea, and Mrs. Tillett then pleaded with Marie for one more song before they had to go back to their room to pack. She agreed and sat at the piano and began to play "Auld Lang Syne." But she could not bring herself to sing it, for fear it would make her cry.

When the song was done, she embraced both the Tilletts. Frances held her very tight for a moment, and said, "I do hope we'll always be friends. Remember, Hitchin is not so very far from Knebworth. If you stay there for a while, perhaps you'll find time to visit us."

"I hope so," Marie said softly, "I really hope so."

CHAPTER SIX

A VISIT TO KNEBWORTH

Before dawn on Easter Monday, Philip and Marie boarded the Great Western Railway train that would take them from Torquay to Paddington, a distance of nearly 200 miles. To help pass the time, Marie had purchased an inexpensive railway edition of A Strange Story, one of Lord Lytton's occult novels. My, it's beautifully written, she thought, if only I could understand what it's all about. Still, just over six hours later, she had read half the book when the train reached Paddington.

There, they had a short wait, as they had to make a connection for the train that would carry them the relatively short distance to Stevenage. Along the way, Marie managed to get a brief but refreshing nap. Philip nudged her awake as the train was entering the

Stevenage station. The low late afternoon sun shone in through the window, and Marie squinted and kept her hand over her face.

Once on the platform, she and Philip began searching for the servant they expected to take them on to Knebworth House. But no one there appeared to be looking for them. "Perhaps his Lordship forgot about us," Philip said, half hoping that might be the case. Marie, now holding the edge of her hand against her forehead to block the glare, spotted a row of horse-drawn carriages just outside the station. "One of those must be from Knebworth."

Right in front of the line was a strikingly beautiful brougham that caught the Deflorettes' attention. The coachman waved to them, and, as they approached, they saw the carriage door open, and puffs of pipe smoke rising from within. "I just can't believe it," Marie whispered to her husband, "he came to fetch us himself." They entered the carriage, and Lord Lytton greeted them warmly. "This must be a most exciting day for you both," he said exuberantly. "I envy you; you're going to see Knebworth for the very first time! But that is the wonder of youth, one constantly experiences new things! It is such a grand time of life: I truly mourn for the loss of my own youth, the golden days, the time of pleasure. If only young people could realize how fortunate they are!"

As the carriage made its way toward his home, Lytton told the Deflorettes stories about the points of interest along the way: a wooded dell that may or may not be inhabited by sprites; an ancient viaduct; and an open field where, he said, "Ten centuries ago, King Alfred the Great fought a famous battle against the Danes in this very spot." Soon, their route took them by a small cottage alongside a stream. An old man, wearing a much-patched coat and holding a fishing pole, was standing with one foot in the stream and the other on the bank. Lytton ordered the coachman to stop.

Alighting from the carriage, Lytton called to the old man, who turned, set down his fishing pole, and came slowly toward him. "Tom, old friend, how are you this fine day?" Lytton said with a warm smile.

"I'm very well indeed, thank you, Sir Edward—oh goodness—I beg pardon—I mean my Lord."

"Never mind that," Lytton said, placing his hand on the old man's shoulder. "We've known each other far too long to worry about such things. Just tell me, Tom, is there anything that you need?"

"Just one thing: a bit more luck with the fish, and then I'll have all I need or want."

"In that case, I'll let you get back to it. Good luck, and stay well, my friend."

"May God bless you, sir, and bless you all your days."

Lytton returned to the carriage and signaled the coachman to proceed. The Deflorettes remained silent, but Lytton perceived they were curious about the old man. "Tom has lived hereabouts all his life. I cannot remember a time when he wasn't around."

The carriage continued on for about four miles on a path bounded on both sides by blossoming hedgerows. Far off to their right, they could see a herd of deer grazing in Knebworth's parkland.

"Something tells me venison may be on the menu some evening this week," Philip said with a hopeful expression.

"I leave such matters to Jackson and to Cook. As there is no Lady—er, that is to say…." Lytton paused for a moment and then mumbled something his companions could not understand. He puffed his pipe a few times and then continued. "We have a new cook, and there's nobody to match her in the gastronomic arts. And, as old Tom could tell you, the trout hereabouts is also very good. And whatever the meal, Jackson makes sure there's a good wine to go with it."

"Look," Marie shouted as she saw in the distance the spires of Knebworth House rising to the sky. Mrs. Tillett was right, she thought to herself. It really is a palace.

There was still a long way to go before they would reach the house, but Marie was utterly unaware of the time that passed or of anything her companions might be saying. The sight of the great house, with its towers and pillars, fully absorbed her attention. When the coachman finally brought the horse to a stop, Marie remained motionless, staring upward at the gargoyles and other manifestations of Gothic imagination that adorned the structure before her.

Lytton thought she might be in a trance. "We've arrived," he told her in a louder-than-usual voice.

"We sure have. We sure have arrived now."

"Don't talk like that," Philip said with a laugh. "You sound like a bumpkin from the backwoods. You've seen big houses before, haven't you?"

"Big, yes. But not like this!"

"She's just worn out from her long journey," Lytton said sympathetically. "Let's go inside, and I'll show you the bedroom you'll use whilst you're here. Don't worry about the bags; James will bring them."

Jackson, who evidently had heard the carriage's approach, was now standing in the open doorway.

"May I offer any assistance to your guests, My Lord?"

"Yes, take care of everything as usual. Except I will show Mr. and Mrs. Deflorette to their room myself. They will use the Queen's Bedroom. They have had a long journey and will need a rest before dinner."

"Very good, my Lord."

Once inside the house, Lytton beckoned the Deflorettes to follow him. Philip did so, but he soon stopped and informed his host that Marie had wandered off somewhere. After a brief search, they found

Marie standing near the foot of the oak stairway leading to the second floor. Although the stairway was
itself remarkable for its carvings and statuary, Marie
stood with her back to it, giving her attention instead
to the suits of armor—about a half dozen of them—
that stood in a row along the opposite wall. Philip and
Lytton exchanged glances. "It looks as if your wife is
busy inspecting the troops," Lytton whispered to his
companion, and then, in a more indulgent tone, continued: "Marie, my dear, I see you've discovered some
of my worthy ancestors. I assure you they played no
ignoble part in our history."

"I never saw anything like this before. Have you,
Philip?" Marie gently tapped an armor breastplate
with her hand. "Why, I feel like we've just stopped off
to pay a visit to the knights of King Arthur's Round
Table."

"Now, you've raised one of my favorite subjects,"
Lytton said. "Did you know my ancestry is in part
Welsh? I relish my kinship with the chivalry of Cymru.
Have either of you read my epic poem, King Arthur?
You haven't? What a pity. It's my favorite of all my
works, though much underappreciated in this prosaic
age. I will gladly leave the verdict to posterity, to the
people of the future who will read it, rather than to the
self-styled 'critics' of today who condemn without reading. Someday, you will both peruse it for yourselves.

Perhaps I will read a few cantos to you some evening by the fire. But now we must continue on to your room."

After they had walked part of the way, another thought struck Marie's memory and imagination. Lytton had said to Jackson, "They will use the Queen's Bedroom." The Queen's Bedroom!

She did her best—though without success—to sound calm. "Why, Lord Lytton, it must have been a truly great occasion when the Queen was your guest here. Even for one so accomplished as yourself, that day must rank among your fondest memories. I was curious, how long ago was she here?"

"Roughly 280 years ago," Lytton said dryly, with only the glint in his eyes disclosing how much he was enjoying the misunderstanding. "I may have inadvertently misled you about the origins of the sobriquet borne by the room where you will presently sojourn. Alas, our beloved sovereign Queen Victoria has not—at least not yet—graced us with her presence. Rather, it was Queen Elizabeth who once slept in the room we now approach. Family tradition tells us that Elizabeth visited here back in 1588—the very year she inspired our Navy to defeat the Armada of Spain. Perhaps she composed the famous speech that she gave on the eve of battle right here in the room you will occupy."

"1588! Think of it, Philip, nearly 300 years ago. I don't believe there's a house that old even in Virginia."

Philip wished he could reprimand Marie for her gushing, but he stifled the impulse because he could tell Lytton loved it.

"Now, Marie," Lytton resumed, "if the date 1588 impresses you, consider this. Knebworth House was actually built in 1492. I'm sure that date carries some significance to you."

"Of course it does. That was the year Columbus discovered America."

"Yes, and precisely when Columbus was opening up a New World, the Lyttons were opening up a new house. And here we are—voila—the Queen's Bedroom. I hope it meets your expectations."

"It does indeed," said Marie, speaking very deliberately as she looked around the room. Most impressive was the enormous four-poster bed of carved oak, the ceiling of oak panels adorned with the royal arms, and the walls decorated with old Gobelin tapestries. "I'm sure the Queen felt right at home here. But for me, it will take a little getting used to."

"I'm sure you both will come to enjoy it, at least once you've gotten some rest. And now I will leave you to do just that."

***

Not until breakfast the next morning did Marie come to terms with the fact that she had not been magically transported to King Arthur's Court, nor to the fortress of the Virgin Queen. She was simply a guest in the house of her husband's employer.

Jackson was extremely courteous to the Deflorettes. "If there is anything you require, I will do my best to meet your needs. We pride ourselves on serving a good breakfast here at Knebworth. Regrettably, his Lordship will not be joining you this morning. I believe he was up very late last night and will remain abed for another hour or more. But it's a good sign. He must be making excellent progress on his new book."

"I'm glad to hear that," Philip said. "I will need to speak with him about that, as well as a number of other items of business. What would be a good time for me to meet with him?"

"His Lordship generally repairs to his study after breakfast and works there until two o'clock. If you would be good enough to speak to me at that hour, I will confirm the appointment with His Lordship, and, if he finds it convenient, I will bring you there. I believe his Lordship would like to show you both around the house. There's so much to see of historical and artistic interest. If you permit me, I suggest that after breakfast, you may wish to explore the grounds and our gardens. It's a lovely day for a walk."

"Excellent suggestion, Mr. Jackson. From the brief view of it we got yesterday, I want to see more of Knebworth Park. Besides, we will need some exercise, lest we grow too fat from enjoying the wonderful breakfast Mrs. Roberts prepared for us. Please convey our sincere thanks to her."

"I will certainly do so, Mr. Deflorette. And thank you."

✦✦✦

After breakfast, Philip and Marie set off on their stroll through Knebworth Park. It was too early in the year to see the gardens at their best; still, there were already daffodils and crocuses in bloom. Many of the flower beds surrounded statuary: images of satyrs and gryphons mingled with angelic figures, an incongruity that reflected Lytton's taste for both the grotesque and the sentimental.

The Deflorettes tramped through a forested area and came across an expanse of short grass that contained an engraved pedestal supporting an urn. Marie's curiosity was piqued, and she examined the structure.

"Why, Philip, it's the grave of Lord Lytton's dog. Listen to what it says here:

Alas Poor Beau
(Died February 28, 1852.)
It is but to a dog this stone
Is inscribed,

Yet what is now left
Within the home of thy Fathers,
O' Solitary Master
That will grieve at thy departure
Or rejoice at thy return.
EBL

"Isn't that beautiful? But oh, so sad. Poor man, he must be so lonely."

"Yes, sometimes lonely, but not always," said Philip. "Anyway, we had best get on with our walk."

While she enjoyed the gardens, Marie soon grew tired and suggested they turn back. But Philip pointed out a cabin a short distance away. "Let's go there. It looks like a place we can rest awhile before making the long trek back to the house."

"Excellent idea. I'm not used to hiking these days. But I wonder if anyone is living there."

"I doubt it. But let's find out."

It was a small wooden cabin, with a heavy roof and low overhanging eaves. It was not occupied. The door was open. Inside, there were no furnishings except one table and two chairs. There was an inkstand on the table.

"Perhaps he comes here to write sometimes when he wants to clear his mind," Philip suggested, "and look, see those fishing poles in the corner? And did you notice that brook just beyond the cabin?"

"Yes. But it seems a long way to walk just to get one's mind clear."

"Well, he told me that in his younger days, he was a great one for long walks. Not so much nowadays, of course."

Marie grew serious for a moment. "What are you going to talk to him about this afternoon?"

"Just about the things we've talked about. Our future. Our return home."

Marie frowned. "I suppose I've had my say on that subject," she said in a tone of resignation. "Let's talk about something else. When are the other visitors going to arrive at Knebworth?"

"Tomorrow afternoon."

"All too soon, in my opinion. I think these days, while we're the only guests, are going to prove the best days of our visit. To be perfectly honest, I don't much care for the others, excepting, of course, our dear Mark."

Philip laughed. "I don't think you have reason to dislike any of the others, with a single exception. It's just Lord Henry Worthing you don't like, isn't it? And you find the rest guilty by association. What about the others? For instance, how do you feel about Lady Henry?"

"Who is Lady Henry?"

"Why, Lord Henry's wife, of course."

"And her name is also Henry?"

"It is since she married Lord Henry."

"I don't get it," Marie said, shaking her head. "When I married you, Philip, I was very happy and proud to take your last name, 'Deflorette.' It's such a beautiful name, especially on a day like this, walking through these lovely gardens, we Deflorettes fit right in. But I sure wouldn't want anyone to call me 'Lady Philip.'"

"Well, that's what I've been telling you all along," Philip said, with the satisfied look of one whose point has just been proven. "We don't really belong here, because we need to have everything explained to us in this country. You should have realized that last year when we went to that little shop in Lamb's Conduit Street, remember?"

"How can I forget it? The man behind the counter said to me, 'Two and six, please.' And I answered, 'eight.'"

"Well, at least your arithmetic was correct."

"Don't sound so surprised. Anyway, it was lucky you were there to hand him the right coins. Even after all this time, I still don't understand the money over here."

"And that's no wonder. We've never had much of it."

Marie looked very serious for a moment. "I may not understand it, but you do. You even understand why some wives take their husbands' first names as well as their last names. In fact, you understand it all, and what you don't know, you can find out. Please remember that when you have your discussion with Lord Lytton this afternoon."

CHAPTER SEVEN

GETTING DOWN TO CASES

At midday, Jackson took a break to relax and enjoy a sandwich in his pantry. He had reached the age when one begins to think of turning to a less strenuous occupation. The notion of finding a situation in a little shop in a seaside resort appealed to him. He enjoyed at least pondering the possibilities.

The cook interrupted his reverie. "Mr. Jackson," she asked in her most genteel tones, "begging your pardon, but I should like to inquire if you 'ave a count of the number of guests at the dinner tomorrow night? One must prepare for an occasion of this importance, as you well know. I fear it may 'ave crept up me."

"No, Mrs. Roberts, I have not made a count. But I believe I could make one right now."

"That would be ever so much appreciated, Mr. Jackson. The sooner I 'ave a count, the better."

"Very well. Let's get right to it. Now, let me see. There's His Lordship, of course, and Mr. and Mrs. Deflorette. That makes three. And then there's-"

"Such a lovely young couple, they are," Mrs. Roberts interrupted. "So very refined. But the name—Deflorette. It's not English, is it? Foreigners, I should say. Perhaps French. It sounds French to me. Are they French?"

"Not at all. They're Americans."

"Americans? Are you sure? I should never 'ave guessed. I've always 'eard that Americans are loud and crude-mannered. The Deflorettes are nothing like that at all. It goes to show, you never can tell."

"I believe they come from the southern states of America. I've been told that people from that region are generally better bred than those from other parts of the country. As I was saying, that makes three-"

"You can also tell from their voices that they're not English. Not English at all. But I should never 'ave took 'em for Americans."

Mr. Jackson, speaking distinctly and louder than before, continued: "And then there's Lord and Lady Henry Worthing—that makes five—and then…"

"Oh yes, I remember the Worthings. They were 'ere last year, as I recall. She's quite a beauty, isn't she?"

"Indeed. Very attractive. Sir William and Lady Carey make seven, Mr. and Mrs. Mark Hornell—that's nine—and then there's…. I can't recall the other gentleman's name at the moment. I know he's a member of the House of Lords…."

"No matter to me where he's a member. All I care about at this moment is that he makes the count number ten."

"Yes, how right you are, Mrs. Roberts. But the count will be at least eleven. Sir Robert Penrod is expected as well."

"And 'is wife?"

"No, unfortunately, Sir Robert is a widower."

"Good 'eavens, there's definitely a shortage of ladies at this dinner. I seem to recall the name, now that you've called it to mind. Sir Robert was 'ere on a prior occasion, I believe. If memory serves, the gentleman is a solicitor."

"Actually, he's a barrister. I may add that at present he is also Sheriff of the county."

"Is that a fact? Well, I'd best be on my best behavior tomorrow," she said with a laugh. "So, is that the lot, then?"

"Possibly. But I think it best that you expect an even dozen. A gentleman called Daniel Holmes will be here tomorrow evening to provide some entertainment for the ladies and gentlemen. I am not sure whether he will be joining the others for dinner or arriving afterward."

"That's just as well, either way. An even dozen is just the right number for the Dining Parlor. Forewarned is forearmed, as they say."

✡✡✡

Philip and Marie had returned to Knebworth House and were resting in the Queen's Bedroom when Jackson came by soon after two o'clock.

"I gave his Lordship your message, sir, and he is most anxious to see you."

Philip took a deep breath, just as one might when about to dive into very cold water.

"Is he awaiting me in his study, Mr. Jackson?"

"No, sir. He's now over in the library. I believe he is doing some research. But he would like to see you as soon as it's convenient."

"Very well."

"Please follow me, sir. I'll show you the way."

Philip gave Marie a kiss. "Wish me luck."

Marie nodded and managed an uneasy half-smile. "You don't need luck, my love."

As they made their way to the library, Jackson occasionally identified the subjects of the portraits that adorned the walls. Philip stopped to take a closer look at one who, according to Jackson, was a Lytton ancestor who had played an important role in the seventeenth-century English Civil War, on the side of the rebels.

"I feel a certain kinship with this fellow," Philip said with a smile, "even though my mother told me her ancestors fought on the side of the Cavaliers."

They reached the hallway containing the suits of armor that had so captivated Marie the day before. Philip imitated her action by gently tapping one of the breastplates.

"This is quite a collection, Mr. Jackson. One never sees anything like it in America."

"You'd be surprised, sir, how many visitors who are native to this country react in just the same way. The Armory is certainly one of the many remarkable features of Knebworth House. And now, sir, we come to a room even more remarkable—the library. I'll announce you and then leave you to your meeting with his Lordship."

Philip entered the library and greeted Lord Lytton, who was seated at a small table in the middle of the room. He had evidently been making notes on a sheaf of paper concerning a book that was lying open on the table. Philip could not help looking away from his employer momentarily to the many bookcases that rose from the floor nearly to the ceiling. On the shelves were hundreds of leather-bound books, some of them obviously very old. Philip sighed and asked if he might be seated.

Lytton smiled. He recognized the dazzled look in Philip's eyes; he had seen it before in the eyes of other well-educated young men who were entering the Knebworth library for the first time. "Not just yet, my boy. You caught me making some notes from this interesting volume. I want to finish what I'm doing before I forget. Old men forget, as you know. Why don't you browse around the library for a few minutes while I finish up what I was about, if you don't mind."

Philip didn't mind. For about fifteen minutes, he strolled about the library, examining the contents of a half dozen bookcases, even using a step ladder to examine the volumes on the upper shelves. He was not surprised to find so many works of classical literature and belle lettres. But he was astonished to see how extensive was Lytton's collection of rare works on occult subjects.

Once Lytton had summoned him to join him at the table, Philip expressed his admiration for the library. "It took me many years to accumulate what you see displayed here," Lytton answered, his expression showing the complacent pride of the successful collector. "I've spent many hours scouring second-hand bookshops, both in this country and on the continent, for antique volumes. I noticed that you took a particular interest in those that may contain answers to mysteries that have baffled philosophers since ancient times. I believe, in several instances, the copy in my possession is the only one, or perhaps one of only two or three, still existing in all the world."

"Remarkable!"

"Indeed, it is. And someday, when we have time, I would like to show them to you. By the way," he asked, handing Philip the book that was on the table, "are you by any chance interested in the subject of the book I've been perusing here today?"

Philip opened the book to the title page. "Elements of Geology by Charles Lyell. No, sir, I'm afraid that is a subject about which I am completely ignorant."

"So are most people, my boy. I'm counting on that fact. I've decided that my new novel—this by the way, is strictly confidential—will be set in the 'center of the earth.' Of course, it will all be imaginary, but I wanted to get some idea of the facts in order to make the fiction more credible."

"That comes as no surprise to me, sir. I learned so much actual history from reading your historical novel, Harold—the Last of the Saxons."

"Yes, I took great pains to make such books as historically accurate as possible. Sir Walter Scott was both a great writer and a fine historian, but he took far too many liberties with the facts, in my opinion." At that, Lytton slapped his hand against the table. "But I didn't send for you to discuss literature. I have some very important news for you."

"Have you, indeed?" asked Philip. He was startled, but too tactful to point out that the meeting was his own idea.

"Yes. Do you know John Gorst?"

"I can't say that I do. Should I?"

"Most certainly. Gorst is the man the Tory party put in charge of the selection of candidates for Parliament. The old, slipshod, catch-as-catch-can practices will no longer do. Since the country adopted democracy back in '67—far too soon in my opinion—we need an organization to select the right men for the right constituencies. And Gorst is the right man to run the party machinery, if you'll excuse that repellent expression."

"That's all quite interesting, sir, but frankly, I fail to see what it has to do with me."

"It has everything to do with you because I plan to recommend your potential candidacy to Gorst. He just sent me a note that a by-election will likely occur next year in a borough in this county. He wants me to suggest a potential candidate. And I want you to know that your name is the one I'm going to suggest."

"I'm afraid, sir, that's quite impossible. I mean, er, I'm honored, of course, terribly honored, that you would think of me in this way. But please give the matter no further consideration. It is simply impossible."

"Oh, you mean because you're not yet a British subject? A mere bagatelle! You'd be surprised how quickly such problems can be resolved, if you know the right people."

"I didn't mean that, sir. I meant I'm not the man for the job. I'm just not."

Lytton shook his head. "It's no wonder you and Marie make such a compatible couple. You both underestimate your respective talents. You won't go far in life if shackled by excessive modesty, a character flaw not to be noticed in myself."

Philip straightened his posture before responding. "It's not that I lack belief in my own abilities. If anything, I overrate them. The fact is—and I regret the necessity of telling you this—I plan to return to America as soon as possible. Before the end of this week, in fact."

"Return to America? Why would you want to do such a thing when you have so many opportunities here? Was I wrong in my opinion that you cherished the ambition to pursue a political career?"

"No, sir, you were not wrong. I am interested in a political career. But I wish to pursue one in my own country. Here, I cannot speak three words without people taking me for a foreigner. But the people back home speak my language."

Lytton leaned back in his chair, his eyes rolling upward, and he responded to Philip in a condescending tone. "My boy," he began, "I realize you have little time to peruse the newspapers, and so you can have no idea of the calamities now roiling your native region. Do you realize that avaricious men from the north, in league with the freedmen, now dominate the southern states? Violent confrontations between these newly powerful forces and your erstwhile compatriots occur all too frequently. There would be little or no opportunity for a man such as yourself in that land of turmoil. On the other hand, if you were to be adopted as the candidate in the borough I mentioned earlier, your course would be clear. The incumbent, who, I have it on good authority, will step down before long, was elected by a huge majority in the Liberal sweep of last year. The borough is normally a competitive one. In a by-election, you could hardly fail to reduce the Liberal majority by an impressive number. You might even win! But, in either case, you would be sure to be the candidate again in the next general election. And, by that time, it is quite likely the tide will have turned in favor of the Tories, and you'll win in a walk."

Philip remained silent for a full minute. His skill as a diplomatist, in which he took such pride, was for once failing him. "All I can say, sir, is to thank you for your kindness," he said at last, "and to say how gratified I am by your evident faith in my abilities. But I have no alternative but to decline the opportunity you have kindly placed before me. I have good and sufficient reasons for my decision. And you must appreciate that, whether right or wrong, I must chart my own course in life."

Lytton persisted in finding Philip's response amusing, albeit puzzling. "Of course, my young friend, I respect your right to make your own decisions. In the full flower of your youth, you are entitled—perhaps even obliged—to make wrong decisions! If I could see that you really do have, as you put it, 'good and sufficient reasons' for returning so abruptly to America, I would encourage you to go and even pay for your passage. But so far, I have not heard a single good reason for doing what you propose."

To Lytton's surprise, Philip stood up and began pacing about the library. At length, he stopped and removed the envelope containing the threatening message from his coat pocket. "I suppose I should tell you the whole story. I had wished to spare you the worry that the contents of this envelope might inflict on you. But I place too high a value on your good opinion of me to continue to hide the truth." He then resumed his seat at the table, handed Lytton the envelope, and related to him how the message had been delivered to him at Torquay.

"Just dreadful," Lytton said after reading the note and listening to Philip's account of its arrival. "Did you contact the police? This threat should have been investigated at once."

"I realize that, but at the time, I was not thinking clearly. I did go to the messenger service, but they could tell me nothing about the individual who sent this to me. I dreaded the publicity that might result from a police investigation, and the embarrassment that might cause you. I decided it would be best to leave the country as soon as I had informed you of the situation. But, when you changed your plans and directed us to remain in Torquay until yesterday, I was, frankly, inclined to board the first ship to America. But Marie had her heart set on visiting Knebworth, and I felt it best to comply with her wishes. I have told her nothing about the threatening note. Her health remains delicate, and I must protect her from any shock."

"I agree with you about that last point. As for the rest, I see no point in belaboring what could or should have been done in the past. We must give our attention to what we should do now."

Philip shifted uneasily in his chair. In his mind, he had already announced what he intended to do and had given the reason why. But his temperament made it impossible for him to argue the point or contradict his employer. "What do you have in mind?" he asked.

Lytton looked thoughtful as he focused his mind on the problem. "The most likely explanation is that this is a prank: some fool's idea of a joke. Still, we must set that point aside. For the present, we must take it au haut sérieux, as the French say. Some day we may think back on this and have a laugh about it. But not now."

Lytton once again read both sides of the paper Philip had handed him. "Whoever wrote this threat may have suspected someone, perhaps you, perhaps me, might recognize his handwriting. He obviously took great pains to disguise it. Come to think of it, the need to disguise his or her identity may account for the use of a piece of a page torn from some journal. The scoundrel may have thought his own writing paper may disclose his own identity in some way."

"If you'll excuse my saying so," Philip said softly, "I doubt that was the reason. The man who wrote this— and I can't believe for a minute any woman would have written it— probably just grabbed the first piece of paper he had to hand. Few people possess distinctive stationery."

"But some do. In fact, many of my friends do. Besides, a literary journal is not something many people just happen to have on hand. They aren't sold at common newsstands. He also had to look through it to find a page that was entirely, or at least mainly, blank. No, some thought went into the selection of this particular paper."

"That may be so," Philip admitted, "but where does that get us?"

"At the moment, it gets us to the other side of this paper, where the poem is printed. Unfortunately, your antagonist left us only a fragment of the verse. To get a sense of it, permit me to read it aloud:

No fear of a crowd; towards the end of the course
They have left behind but a handful of horse.
To keep at their side on the gods one must call
For the wind of a tutor of -

"Not bad, as far as it goes. Don't you agree, Philip?"

"Not much to go on there. I don't even know what it means."

Lytton pointed to the bottom of the note. "Look here. The tear is not straight. The person who sent this intentionally tore the paper upward at this point, in order that the last word or words of the line would not be revealed. It may well be that he did not want you to see the end of the line because it might give a hint of his identity. Let me think: it's most probably a word that rhymes with 'call.'"

"There are many of those."

"You're right. Let's leave the matter of the poem for a moment and discuss—no, wait. I think I've seen this verse before, somewhere."

"Does it matter? If you've seen it, thousands of others have as well."

"You have a logical mind, Philip. But sometimes one must rely on instinct rather than logic. I have a feeling that if I could remember where this poem was published, it might give us a clue as to the identity of the person who sent it. I know I've seen it. Oh, if only I retained the powers of memory I enjoyed in my youth!"

"It will come to you, I'm sure. But you were saying we should leave the poem and discuss something else."

"Quite right. You do make an excellent secretary, no doubt about it. But the 'something else' is not a pleasant topic. To put it bluntly, do you have any idea who in England might want so badly for you to quit this realm that he would go so far as to threaten murder?"

The question took Philip aback. It now seemed such an obvious line of inquiry that he wondered why he had never even considered the matter before. He had just wanted to get away. Perhaps, he said to himself, I'm really just a coward.

"I really have no idea, Lord Lytton. I've always done my best to get along with everyone. To my knowledge, I've not an enemy in the world."

"Well," Lytton responded, trying not to sound too flippant, "I reckon you have at least one. Recall that you served the Southern cause in a very bitter Civil War. Have you encountered anyone over here from the opposing side who might have nurtured his enmity toward you?"

"I don't think so. In the activities I was called upon to perform, one did not seek interaction with the Yankees. The only one of the latter I ever had words with was a young man called Henry Adams, the son of the U.S. Minister to this country. But that was long ago, and he didn't strike me as the violent type."

"Well, then, how about the violent types on your own side? After all, the Confederacy did not carry the day. In the shadow of defeat, there are likely to be recriminations, often bitter recriminations, among those on the losing side."

Philip pondered the question for a moment. "No, I don't think so. We were all loyal to one another as well as to the cause we served. We gladly gave the best we had and only drew closer together when it all came to an unhappy end. Besides, nearly all my comrades have gone either to the continent or back to America."

"We seem to have come up to another blank wall. But a very troubling thought occurs to me, as I'm sure it has to you. The threatening note is addressed to 'Deflorettes.' Plural. That little 's' at the end means our dear little Marie is included in the threat."

"Yes, sir, it does mean just that. I hope that accounts for my anxiety to leave England."

Lytton ignored that last remark and continued his effort to identify any possible suspect. "Did she antagonize anyone over here? Is it possible she made some enemies? What do you know of the people she's passed her time with while you were busy at work?"

Philip shook his head. "She knew, during the war, that my work was confidential, and she kept herself pretty much to herself. Then she became very ill for a while, as you have heard, and saw virtually no one but her doctor. And you know pretty much what she was doing in Torquay."

"But there she often went out during the day."

"Oh yes, of course, you're right about that. But her only friends were a couple of women who were staying at Miller's Hotel: a middle-aged widow and her spinster daughter. But they seemed as harmless as any-one could be."

"Perhaps. But it's the harmless-seeming people who are often the most dangerous."

"I very much doubt that's true, at least in this case."

"Then we move on. Are you quite sure Marie had no friends of her own in the Confederate service?"

"Quite sure. Oh, wait a moment. Speaking of Miller's Hotel and the Confederate service reminded me of something I'd forgotten. Now, I don't think it's important, but I suppose I should mention it. Last year, around Christmas, Marie had a chance encounter with an old friend of ours named Monty Kelly. I hadn't seen him since before the war. He happened to be at the hotel, heard Marie playing the piano, and came over to have a chat with her. I had no idea what he did in the war. But he told Marie that he had served in the Confederate Navy."

"Interesting. What was this fellow Kelly doing over here in this country?"

"He had served on the C.S.S. Alabama. After the Alabama was sunk, Kelly was lucky enough to be res-cued and brought to England. Apparently, he has re-mained here ever since."

"Doing what?"

"That I don't know."

"Did either of you meet up with Kelly again after this chance meeting at Christmas?"

"No. But Marie told me her friends, that widow and spinster I mentioned to you already, may have seen him at Miller's Hotel. Marie gave them a colorful description of Kelly. They said they saw someone who looked like the man she described, except that he didn't speak with an American accent. But I'd wager it was he. Kelly had actually been born in Ireland; he came to America with his family as a child to escape the Potato Famine. When I knew him in college, there was still a hint of Irish in his voice."

"That may be significant."

"I don't see how. But, going back to that note I gave you, what puzzles me is what is meant by the phrase 'before the end of Easter.' If it means Easter Sunday, the deadline has already passed. If it means Easter Week, we have just a few days before the time expires. I hope you understand my anxiety about this."

"I do, indeed. By the way, Philip, do you recall the name Colonel Fielding?"

"Certainly. He was mentioned in that rather disturbing letter you got last year from Gathorne Hardy. I've heard you speak of him a few other times."

"Yes. He's a very good man to have around. He's the head of the detective department, you see. Tell you what: I'm going to send an urgent message to him, asking him to come to Knebworth just as soon as he can get away. I think this entire matter should be handed over to him."

Philip sighed. "I hope he gets here soon."

"Don't you worry," Lytton said, placing his hand on Philip's shoulder. "You have a few days before having to make a final decision. In the meanwhile, we'll get to the bottom of this."

CHAPTER EIGHT

THE GATHERING OF THE CLAN

While Lytton did his best to project a calm confidence in his talk with Philip, the death threat had badly frayed the nerves of the aging novelist. He had great difficulty focusing on his literary work that night. When Jackson entered Lytton's bedroom the following morning at eight o'clock, he noted that of the seven cigars that had been placed on the nightstand the previous evening, only two had been smoked.

"Good morning, m'Lord," Jackson said in the stentorian tones he always used to awaken his somewhat hard-of-hearing employer.

Lytton was slow to come fully to consciousness. "I'm too ill to leave this room, Jackson," he said at last in a hoarse whisper intended to elicit sympathy. "I shall remain abed all day. No, wait. I cannot. Visitors are coming today, a veritable legion of them. Still, I am too weak to move."

"Shall I send for Dr. Baker, sir?" said Jackson in a correct, business-like voice.

"Yes. Immediately. No, wait. All those guests. All those people. Perhaps I'll feel better once I've eaten. Have James bring my breakfast in here. A small breakfast. I'll remain here until noon. At least until noon. If I feel up to it, I shall repair to my study around one o'clock. Is that understood?"

"Yes, indeed, m'Lord."

"Now, about the guests. I will not be able to greet any of them. You must meet them and escort them to their rooms. But I will not see anyone until dinner time. Is that clear?"

"Yes, m'Lord."

"Except for Lord Henry Worthing. I wish to speak with him as soon as he arrives. Understood?"

"It will be done, just as you say."

"Oh, and one more thing. Send around a message to Dr. Baker. Tell him I was unwell this morning but began to feel better. But he is to come here tonight, lest I take a turn for the worse. He must come here without fail. Is that understood?"

"Yes, m'Lord. I will see to it at once."

✵✵✵

Marie slept late that morning. Her long walk of the previous day had worn her out. Once she finally awakened, she found a note Philip had left for her, saying that he had already had breakfast and was spending the remainder of the morning going through Lytton's correspondence. Marie did not mind. The previous evening, she was pleased with Philip's report of his talk with Lord Lytton. His version of the conversation omitted a great deal. He only told her that he had spoken of his intention to return to America and that Lytton had urged him to defer a final decision for a couple of days until they could have a further discussion. Marie expected that Lytton's inventive mind could conjure up some way of persuading Philip that he should remain in England.

By midday, Marie was comfortably settled in one of the parlors, continuing her reading of A Strange Story. From her location, she could hear Jackson greeting the various guests as they arrived. But she kept herself out of sight until she recognized the voice of Mark Hornell. She also heard the loud voice of a woman, giving instructions to the servants. Marie guessed it must be the voice of Mark's wife, whom she had never met. Marie then immediately put down her book and hurried out to welcome the Hornells.

Mark greeted her warmly and made the introductions. "I'd like you to meet my wife, Gladys. Gladys, meet Marie Deflorette."

"How do you do, Mrs. Hornell? I'm so pleased to meet you at last."

"How do you do? So, you're the famous Marie I've heard so much about." Somehow, Mrs. Hornell's tone made her words sound like a rebuke.

"I look forward to getting to know you, Mrs. Hornell. May I call you Gladys?"

Mrs. Hornell ignored the question. "We will get to know one another. I understand you've been here at Knebworth for some time already. Have you learned where the patio is located?" Marie nodded. "Then we shall take tea there in one hour," Mrs. Hornell said, as if issuing a command.

"That sounds very nice," Mark interjected.

"I mean tea for Mrs. Deflorette and myself. You must find something else to occupy your time and not be in the way."

Marie was taken aback by this remark. Mark is a highly respected political journalist, she said to herself, but his wife speaks to him as if he were a wayward six-year-old.

"An hour from now—suits me fine. It may give me time to finish reading A Strange Story. I only wish I were smart enough to understand it."

"You need not bother," said Mrs. Hornell, as she and Mark began following Jackson's lead on the way to their bedroom. "It's one of Lytton's less impressive efforts."

Marie returned unhappily to the parlor where she had been reading the book. She had looked forward to meeting Mark's wife, expecting they would become great friends. Now crestfallen, Marie wondered how such a fine man as Mark could have such an unpleasant woman for a wife. Could Gladys have been attractive in her youth? She certainly wasn't now: with her narrow, hawk-like face and her steel-gray hair, she looked years older than her husband.

After reading for a little while, Marie put the book aside and began to consider how she could make the best of things. What would Philip do in a case like this? She had witnessed Philip ameliorate many an awkward social situation. Certainly, she could replicate his methods after so many years. She devoted the remainder of the hour to pondering how Philip would behave if he were having tea with someone as unpleasant as Gladys Hornell. Marie vowed to conduct herself accordingly.

She checked the clock in the parlor to make sure an hour had passed, and then waited a further ten minutes, so that she would not arrive too soon. Once she finally appeared on the patio, she was not displeased to note that Mrs. Hornell looked irritated at being kept waiting.

"It's so good to see you again, Mrs. Hornell, and thank you so much for inviting me. My, what a beautiful spot we have here with a wonderful view of the garden and the flowers, and such a lovely day to be outdoors!"

Mrs. Hornell was obviously well drilled in the rituals of serving tea and played the part of hostess. "Such excellent tea," Marie said after taking her first sip. "Thank you so much."

"I can hardly take credit for that. I did not prepare it, after all."

"Oh, didn't you? By the way, did you happen to observe the herd of deer as you drove through Knebworth Park? Magnificent, aren't they?"

"Mrs. Deflorette, I must tell you that I believe in plain talk. I didn't invite you to have tea with me in order to discuss either the weather or the flora and fauna of Knebworth Park. I have important matters to discuss, matters of great importance for you and for your future."

"Have you, indeed? I should be most interested."

"I must say that you're not at all the kind of woman I expected. You seem entirely oblivious of your situation. It is therefore all the more important to tell you in no uncertain terms that you are in a most perilous position."

Marie was both amused and annoyed. But she adhered to Philip's dictum that a diplomat must use words to disguise thoughts. She responded in as pleasant a tone as she could manage. "I very much appreciate your warning me of this peril. Please do go on."

"I realize it is possible that you are not even aware of the danger that is quite likely to destroy your life. You are a young woman and no doubt ignorant of the ways of the world. Perhaps you are even unaware of Lytton's reputation where women are concerned."

"I am unaware of that. Besides, what does Lord Lytton's reputation have to do with me?"

"It is your reputation I'm talking about, not his. Your conduct has been whispered about all over London. A young, pretty girl like yourself, living in his house in Torquay, and now here at Knebworth. Of course, I blame myself, at least in part. This started at that dinner last year at Rockbridge House. I had intended to go. Lord Burnley gives such excellent dinners. But I had a stupid headache, so I stayed home. Had I been there, I should have nipped this business in the bud."

"If by 'this business,' you mean Philip's becoming Lord Lytton's secretary, I must inform you, since you were unfortunately absent due to your headache, that it was your own husband who suggested that my husband take on that job. Mark obviously saw nothing wrong in it."

"Mr. Hornell never sees anything of real consequence. His head is full of nonsense. He only thinks about what the government of the day may be doing, who will get what ministerial post, or how the Tories may finally win some silly election. He is not a man of the world."

"I trust that you do realize I was not living alone with Lord Lytton at Torquay. My husband was there, just as he is here at Knebworth now."

Mrs. Hornell shook her head in exasperation. "You have no idea, do you, about the workings of the real world. Appearances are what matter, regardless of what is actually happening. Besides, husbands can be very complaisant creatures, especially ambitious ones. Your husband is assumed to be complaisant. He is ambitious, isn't he?"

Marie was finding the role of a diplomat to be more difficult than she had expected. "Well, my husband is certainly, to put it in your own terms, a man of the world. But I don't see why my husband's ambitions should be of any concern to you."

"I am concerned because your husband is associated with my husband, and if your husband is involved in scandal, it will sully my husband's reputation and perhaps even affect my own."

"Well, since you've obviously had more experience with such matters than I have had, may I ask what you would suggest I do about all this?"

"Isn't it obvious? You and your husband should leave England immediately. Go back to America. Go to France. Go anyplace where your relationship with Lytton is not known."

Marie stood up. "I thank you for your suggestion. Believe me, I shall discuss the idea with my husband.

But for now, I'm going back inside to finish A Strange Story. By the way, you remind me very much of one of the characters in it, and, if you really have read the book, you'll know which one I mean. Thanks again for the tea. We must do this again soon. Good day, Gladys."

While Marie was on the patio, Jackson was showing Lord and Lady Henry Worthing, who had just arrived, to the bedroom they would use during their stay at Knebworth.

"I wish you to know, Lord Henry, that, although Lord Lytton was not feeling well this morning, he nonetheless instructed me to request that you call upon him in his study as soon as may be convenient. He is most anxious to see you, sir."

"Thank you, Jackson. You have saved me the trouble of inquiring as to when it might be convenient for me to call upon him. I shall saunter over to the study within the hour."

"Very good, sir."

Later that afternoon, Lord Henry arrived at the study and found Lytton in a relaxed posture, smoking a pipe six feet long.

"You are looking well, sir," Lord Henry remarked. "Smoking seems to agree with you. I've noticed over the years that you smoke a good deal."

"No, indeed, I do not. I just take a few whiffs and then put my pipe down. But I do find that tobacco soothes my nerves. That's a necessity in these troubled times."

"Well, here's some political news that you might also find soothing." Lord Henry paused briefly, for dramatic effect, and then launched his report. "Old Fisher is going to give up his seat next year. After spending ten years in the House without ever opening his mouth, he has finally run out of things not to say. I have heard this from three discrete sources."

Lytton shook his head. "Your sources were, in fact, indiscreet. I understand John Gorst wishes to keep this development quiet until he has found an appropriate candidate."

"Then there's no doubt that the report is true. I can imagine the sort of candidate Gorst is seeking," Lord Henry added wryly. "Someone who achieved a brilliant record at university, and whose wit shines in the best society. In short, a man who combines the best attributes of Gladstone and of Disraeli, respectively."

"Actually, he's looking for a man with the attributes of Don Quixote: someone willing to expend his energy tilting at windmills. Old Fisher made no mark in the House of Commons, as you observe, but even he carried the constituency by a substantial majority in the last election. If such a nonentity as he could do that, it's safe to assume the Liberals will hold the seat with anyone else. Our candidate should be someone so lacking in political prospects that even a resounding defeat would not lessen them. In fact, I may suggest my private secretary, Mr. Deflorette, to make the contest."

"You mean the American? But he ...."

"Oh, I know what you're going to say," Lytton interrupted. "We would need a British subject. That won't matter. It's not as if he's actually going to win the seat."

"Oh, I begin to understand," said Lord Henry, trying to paper over his disappointment. "We need someone who wants the honor of being nominated but shuns the risk of being elected. But, to my mind, there's not much point to becoming a candidate without a fair prospect of success; and with success, by dint of membership in the Commons, one would enjoy the privilege of being no longer susceptible to arrest for debt."

"You have it precisely. While we're on the subject, I want you to know that I plan to mention your name to Gorst whenever a safe seat should come open. You belong in the House, my friend, and I'm sure you will be selected as a candidate in the next general election. It can be no more than six years away. But actually, I wanted to talk with you today, not about politics, but about literature."

"Literature? Why, have you heard of a publisher in search of an author?"

"No—oh, Lord Henry, you never fail to amuse me. I thank you for that. Here is the thing: some lines of poetry keep running through my mind. But for the life of me, I cannot remember who wrote them or where I read them. It's really a frustration, and you're my only hope for relieving it."

"I feel my knowledge of poetry is much less than your own; but, nothing ventured, nothing gained. Pray, recite the line just as it runs through your mind."

Lytton tried to comply from memory: "'No fear of a crowd; towards the end of the course. They have left all behind but a handful of horse.' Something, Something. 'One must call for the wind of a tutor,' something, something, that's all. Does it sound familiar?"

Lord Henry half closed his eyes and gazed upward. He then began repeating some of the words, as if trying to summon a recollection. "Left all behind but a handful of horse ... A handful of horse." Then he smiled broadly as the recollection arrived. "Lord Lytton, you didn't give me much to go on. Nonetheless, I have the answer. Sometimes I astonish even myself."

"Indeed, Lord Henry, I was certain you would be the one person who could do it. Please proceed, if you would be so kind."

"Those lines are from a poem written in honor of the Cambridge oarsmen about a decade ago. I should, of course, like to leave you in awe of my ready memory and vast erudition. But, in truth, it happens that I was there at the time, and that is the only reason I recognize it. The only reason. The author was a chap called George Otto Trevelyan. He was a contemporary of mine at Trinity College. By the way, George is a nephew of the late Lord Macaulay, a great friend of yours, as I believe you have mentioned on occasion."

"Yes, and Macaulay was likewise at Trinity, as was Sir Robert Penrod."

"As you were yourself, I believe."

"Your memory is imperfect on that point, Lord Henry. While I did begin at Trinity, I moved on to Trinity Hall. Trinity Hall! Yes, that's it. That would complete the rhyme."

"You mean in George's poem? I don't know it by heart. But I suspect Trinity Hall comes in there somewhere. There are lots of Cambridge references in it, lots of jokes inscrutable to all but Cambridge men. It was rather well done, I would say. I believe, if my imperfect memory may be relied upon, it appeared in Macmillan's. If interested, you might locate the back issue at some college library."

"Speaking of colleges," Lytton remarked, "we will have quite a gathering of Cambridge men here this evening. You and Sir Robert from Trinity, I from Trinity Hall, and Lord Burnley, who was at King's. All this talk of Cambridge has made me nostalgic and wishing to revisit my old haunts. I wonder what's going on there now."

"A great deal, I should imagine. The Easter Term has just begun."

"Oh, that's right, Lord Henry. The Easter Term! I had forgotten about that. In fact, Easter won't come to an end until June. For some reason, that makes me very happy. This night we shall have a lovely dinner!"

CHAPTER NINE

A DINNER AT
KNEBWORTH HOUSE

April, 1869

Later that afternoon, Jackson instructed James, the
footman, to call on each of the guests and convey Lord
Lytton's request that they gather in the Banqueting
Hall at seven o'clock that evening. Lytton had selected
that particular venue because it contained a piano,
and he had planned a musical entertainment before
dinner. Shortly after the appointed hour, he observed
Cora, Lady Carey, shambling into the Hall, violin case
in hand.

"Lady Carey," he said in his most genial manner,
"we are delighted that you have consented to entertain
us this evening. I have been looking forward to this for

weeks. Pray, begin your performance whenever ready but not later than 7:15. Latecomers will be out of luck."

"Aye, I shall be ready presently. Will someone be accompanying me on that piano?"

"I will try to persuade Mrs. Deflorette to do so."

As Lytton expected, Marie was initially reluctant. She pointed out the difficulty of accompanying a violinist when one has no idea what music she intends to play and therefore has had no opportunity to prepare. She doubted she would be equal to the task. But Lytton insisted that he had greater confidence in her ability than she had herself. Realizing there was no alternative, Marie finally agreed and asked Lady Carey what piece she had chosen to perform.

"Schumann's Violin Sonata No. 1 in A minor. I've been hard at it for weeks and finally have it memorized. But I didn't think to bring the sheet music. I'm sorry. Rather thoughtless of me. Do you think you can get by without it?"

"I don't know. But I suppose I can always ad lib, if necessary," Marie said, trying to sound confident. "Go ahead and tune your violin and just give me a nod when you're ready to begin."

When Cora and Marie first began to play, the other guests stood and listened attentively. But the performance of Schumann's lilting melodies consumed over a quarter hour. Gradually, the audience dispersed into small groups of conversationalists, spread about the enormous Banqueting Hall. When the music stopped, there was no applause.

"Well, my dear Mrs. Deflorette," Cora said in hushed tones, "contrary to all expectations, it turned out you were the one who knew your part, and I the one who needed to ad lib. I know when I'm outclassed. I felt like a plater sent out to run the Derby."

"No, you did very well, Lady Carey. Shall we try another?"

"No one would notice if we did. But, please, perform something on your own. No doubt you have a considerable repertoire at your command. As my husband would say, fire away at will!"

Marie then began an energetic selection from Les Preludes by Franz Liszt. She had played about half of it when interrupted by James's calling out, "Dinner is served!" Marie was glad to have an excuse to stop. The performance had left her both physically tired and emotionally spent. She remained seated, her chin resting on her chest, as she stretched and flexed her weary fingers.

She soon became aware of someone, now standing close by her, who was exclaiming, "Brilliant! brilliant!" Marie looked up at a face and flowing blonde tresses that made her think of the Madonna by Botticelli.

It took a moment for Marie to recognize the woman congratulating her. "Oh, thank you so much, er, I mean, thank you, Lady Henry."

"Oh, call me Daffy. All my friends do. That 'Lady Henry' stuff is for formal occasions. I'm sure all these titles, sir this and sir that, lord this and lady that, must seem awfully silly to you. And you're absolutely right!"

"Well, I do try to respect the traditions of the country. It's only polite, since I'm a newcomer here. Still, it all does seem strange to me. At least it does sometimes. How did you get the name 'Daffy?'"

"For exactly the reason you think! Well, I suppose the fact that my Christian name is 'Daphne' may have played a small part in it also. That truly was a wonderful performance. I had no idea!"

"You're very kind, um, Daffy."

"That's the stuff! Say, you must be exhausted. Here you are, a nice glass of champagne. Nothing better to pick you up. Join me in a toast?"

"Certainly."

"To old friends and new!"

"To old friends and new!"

"And now, to dinner!"

✲✲✲

The dinner was sumptuous. It included potato and leek soup, fish, lamb cutlets with asparagus, veal in sauce, and venison with mustard and vegetables. For dessert, there was sponge cake and rice pudding, followed by a cheese course. Service was à la française:

all the courses were placed at the same time on a side table, from which the guests could select whatever they wished. This arrangement required the guests to go back and forth until they had selected everything they wanted. All the while, James stood by to fill and refill the wine glasses, offering a choice of claret, madeira, and champagne.

Early in the proceedings, Philip managed to whisper into Marie's ear, kissing it unobtrusively as he did so: "You were magnificent as always, my love. I know you're hungry, but be careful not to overdo it. Take a little of everything, but not too much of anything." Marie shrugged in response: easier said than done.

The conversation lagged until the diners were largely settled. Mrs. Hornell's voice was loud enough to be heard above the din of serving dishes and cutlery. "Lord Lytton, it seems to me it has been a good many years since you've managed to produce a new novel. How long must we wait for the next one?"

"Indefinitely, madam, indefinitely. Given my age and the uncertain state of my health, it may well be that I have placed my last production before an altogether too unappreciative public."

"I find that difficult to believe," Mrs. Hornell responded. "Mr. Deflorette, you are in service here, I believe, as Lord Lytton's private secretary. Surely you are in a position to enlighten us as to the true state of your recalcitrant employer's literary work."

"I entirely agree with you, Mrs. Hornell," Philip said in an ingratiating manner. "It has indeed been too long since the appearance of A Strange Story. But I have good news for you and for everyone. A new book will come out this year. Lord Lytton's translation of The Odes and Epodes of Horace will soon be published, probably in September or October. I know, Mrs. Hornell, you will enjoy reading it. Indeed, I'm certain it will prove very popular. You should get in touch with Blackwood's soon and reserve a first edition of the book."

"I entirely concur with Mr. Deflorette concerning the probable popularity of this translation," Lord Henry Worthing interjected. "I was privileged to peruse an advance copy of the work, and I assure you it is not intended exclusively for classical scholars."

"I thank you for that, Lord Henry," Lytton said, with a pleased expression. "And since I have no wish to be perceived as recalcitrant, I will disclose a bit of literary news that no one else in the world knows. Recently, as I walked through the halls of this House, I had an inspiration. I will republish, with a new introduction, intended for the rising generation in which we all place such great hopes, my epic poem, King Arthur! Please keep this news to yourselves until all the arrangements have been made with the publishers."

"That's excellent news, sir," said Mark. "I'm certain that this edition will achieve the success the original issue was unfairly denied. I'm trying to recall, when was it that King Arthur was originally published?"

"It was back in '48, I believe," Lytton responded, sounding unable to comprehend such a passage of time. "That was very long ago."

"Indeed, it was," said Sir William Carey, who had hitherto given all his attention to the champagne in his glass and the serving of fish on his plate. "I well recall the upheavals of 1848. It was no time to introduce a work of imagination."

Lady Carey hastened to contextualize her husband's comment. "Aye, no doubt that was the reason your work did not receive the reception it merited, Lord Lytton. That was when revolution was the order of the day."

"But it might be truly said that we are now once again living in a time of upheaval," Mark responded. "Gladstone seems bound and determined to disestablish the Church of Ireland. He, of course, has the votes in the Commons to push through his bill. I wonder if there's any possibility the Lords will block it."

"No possibility at all," said Lord Burnley. "Oh, there may be some quibbling about the financial details, but as for disestablishment itself, the great majority in our House have no stomach to fight the government on this issue. You may be sure that this is just the first round in Gladstone's campaign to pacify Ireland."

"And a futile campaign it will prove. Mark my words," insisted Sir William Carey.

"At this point, I feel obliged to intervene," said Sir Robert Penrod, "lest I overhear some Tory stratagems not intended for my ears. Some of you do not know me very well, or even at all. It is therefore only sporting that I make clear that I am a very decided Liberal and a fervent supporter of Mr. Gladstone. In fact, I became a good friend of Lord Lytton's many years ago when he and I were on the same side of the political fence. I am proud to say our friendship has not waned one iota despite his going over to the Tories."

The ensuing discussion was halted by the piercing voice of Gladys Hornell. "If you gentlemen insist on talking politics, please have the good manners to defer it until we ladies have finished dinner and have withdrawn. You can then bore yourselves silly over your brandy and cigars."

"Oh, Mrs. Hornell, let me reassure you on that point," said Lytton good-naturedly. "There will be tonight no more talk of politics, nor any brandy or cigars, and certainly no boredom. Once dinner is done, we, one and all, shall repair to the Oak Drawing Room, where there will soon arrive Mr. Daniel Holmes, one of the most remarkable men of our age. He will tonight conduct a séance that will both astonish and delight you—or, perchance, terrify you. But it is certain, this will be a night none of you will ever forget."

At this point, Lord Henry Worthing looked upward at the ceiling and began to say, "But we will do our best," until a sharp look from his wife caused him to modify his remark to, "but we will do our best to make welcome whatever spirits may make known their presence this very night."

CHAPTER TEN

A WAY TO THE OTHER WORLD

Fully satiated, the guests withdrew to the Oak Drawing Room. Soon afterward, Daniel Holmes, a young man, about thirty years of age, was ushered into the room by Jackson. Lytton proceeded to introduce him to each of the guests. Marie, once she met Holmes, could not help thinking it laughable that Lytton had described him as "one of the most remarkable men of our age." Why, she thought, there's nothing remarkable about this man. He's short, paunchy, and certainly not handsome. His hair wants combing, and that wispy blonde mustache does nothing for him. Why, if I passed him on the street, I would not give him a second glance.

Philip noted the same qualities but drew a different conclusion. He had expected the medium would have a highly theatrical personality, perhaps wear a top hat and sport a cape, while spouting prophecies in a melo-dramatic manner. Instead, there appeared a plainly dressed, soft-spoken gentleman who had simply come to perform a service. In conversation, Holmes exuded sincerity. When Philip proffered an apology on behalf of fellow guests whose vocal skepticism bordered on rudeness, Holmes brushed the matter aside.

"Encountering doubters is all in a day's work for me. I should find it strange if there were none about. All I ask of them is that, when the time comes, they sit aside while I try to do my job. Curious thing is, on occasions when I have been unsuccessful in making contact with my control, it is the skeptics who complain the most loudly! In any event, I hope I shall succeed to-night in communing with the Afterworld, and thereby not disappoint the doubters, or, of course, those who come with an open mind."

"Well, I assure you my wife and I are as open-minded as anyone," said Philip. "If you don't mind my saying so, I could not help noticing your accent. Are you an American?"

"Yes, I reside in Hartford, Connecticut. And yourself?"

"North Carolina."

"May I then shake your hand, as a fellow countryman?"

"Yes, indeed! I assure you, I am no longer fighting the war."

Holmes looked thoughtful. "You strike me as a capable fellow, Mr. Deflorette. Lord Lytton introduced you as his private secretary. May I call upon you for secretarial assistance during tonight's séance?"

"I don't know. In what way?"

Holmes beckoned Philip over to a round table that had been placed in the center of the Oak Drawing Room.

"As you can see, Mr. Deflorette, the chart placed on this table contains all the letters of the alphabet. A spirit may communicate from the beyond by spelling out the words of a message. Once we've begun, it will be clear to you how that is accomplished. But I'd like you to write down the letters that will form the words. There will be, I trust, conversation between some of us here in this room and the spirits of those who have gone before. I have learned that, after it is over, people are frequently so excited, even overwrought, that they cannot remember what was said. I would very much appreciate it if you could keep an accurate record of the exchanges so that they might be read afterward. A written record would remove all doubt about what took place."

"But won't it be dark in here once we've begun?"

"Yes, but there'll be a single lamp giving off just enough light for us to view the chart and for you to see the paper on which you will record everything that's been said or, rather, everything that's been communicated."

"In that case, it should not be too difficult. Certainly, I'll be glad to help, if I can." Despite his claim to have an open mind, Philip did not believe for a moment that Holmes could actually "commune with the Afterworld." But he was nonetheless persuaded that Holmes honestly believed he possessed a gift that would enable him to do so.

Once the introductions were completed, Lytton went about the room, inviting the guests to take their seats at the round séance table. Only six of the guests came to the table. After seeking others in vain, Lytton told the group that, "it appears Hornell and Burnley have wandered off somewhere; no doubt they're talking politics, perhaps conspiring against the government and do not wish to be overheard. And I have very reluctantly excused Sir William and Lord Henry from participating. Naughty skeptics, they will sit in the corner on the other side of the room."

Holmes took his seat directly opposite Philip. Also seated were Marie, Cora Carey, Lady Henry Worthing, and Gladys Hornell. Holmes asked each of them to say their names, so he could be sure he had them memorized. When Lytton took his seat, that made a total of seven at the table.

"I much prefer to have an even number of men and women," said the medium. "There are seats at the table for eight. Can we not enlist another gentleman to join us?"

Lytton looked about the room and noticed that Sir Robert Penrod was standing some distance away by himself.

"Oh, Sir Robert, please come and take this seat," said Lytton. "Your presence will not only even out the sides, but it will also assure that all political parties are represented."

Sir Robert approached the table but then stopped short. "Under different circumstances, I should be very interested in participating. But I must think of the office I now hold. As Sheriff, I may someday be called upon to arrest young Mr. Holmes here. I would not want my impartiality to be put into question." All, except Holmes, found this excuse quite amusing.

"Well, I guess it's up to me to keep the boat from rocking," said Lady Henry, beckoning her husband to fill the empty seat. "Come over here, Henry. Who knows but that you might make contact with Socrates and finally get answers to all those questions that have perplexed you ever since Eton."

More than a little skeptically, Lord Henry came to the table and glanced at the alphabet chart. "Alas, no Greek letters. I suppose we'll have to call upon Virgil instead. Omnia vincit amor, et nos cedamus amori."

"How true, Lord Henry," said Lytton. "Ladies, permit me to offer a loose translation: You can't beat love, so it's best you knuckle under." He then gave a hand signal to James, the footman, who brought a small lamp and placed it by the table, and then proceeded to extinguish all other lights in the room.

"We must now concentrate," said Holmes softly.

The group of eight sat silently in semi-darkness for what seemed an eternity, although it was really only fifteen minutes. Holmes appeared to have drifted into a trance. Suddenly, everyone else was startled as the table rocked back and forth twice.

"Rosalie, is that you?" Holmes asked in a calm voice, sounding as if he had recognized a friend walking down the street. "Rap once for yes, twice for no."

A single rap was plainly heard. Philip stared hard at Holmes in the dim light. But there was nothing to suggest that the medium had moved any part of his body. In fact, the rapping sound did not even seem to come from his side of the table. Philip wondered, could Holmes really have contacted the "control?"

"Rosalie, I am happy you are with us this evening. Are you happy?"

A single rap. [Yes.]

Holmes then looked around the table. "Rosalie," he asked, "is there someone there who has a message for anyone here with me this day?"

[Yes.]

"Is it for one of the ladies who are present?"

[No.]

"Is it for Mr. Philip Deflorette?"

[No.]

"For Lord Henry Worthing?"

[No.]

"For Lord Lytton, then?"

[Yes.]

"Who is there?"

There was a pause, as if another person were making his way to the rostrum. Then the table rocked back and forth again. Holmes apparently took this as his cue to begin pointing at letters on the chart. He had to go through fifteen letters before a rap indicated that "O" was the first letter of the first word. Holmes was obviously well practiced in the technique, and it did not take long before Philip had recorded the first words on his pad:

"O-l-d b-o-o-k-s-e-l-l-e-r."

Holmes looked toward Philip and asked, "Did it spell 'old bookseller?'" Philip nodded.

Holmes then turned to Lytton. "Have you questions for old bookseller, Lord Lytton?"

"I do indeed." As they proceeded, Philip recorded the questions and answers in his notes:

Q. Did you sell books in London?

A. Reluctantly, yes.

Q. Where in London?

A. Covent Garden.

Q. When did you last do so?

A. Long ago. Who keeps track of time?

Q. I understand. What is your name?

A. You don't remember?

Q. As you said, it was long ago, and I am no longer young.

A. Drotz.

Q. Oh, Mr. Drotz! Are you happy?

A. Yes. You made good use of my books.

Q. I did?

A. I did not wish to part with them. I loved my books. But books would do me no good now.

Q. Which ones did you love the most?

There was a long silence. "I think he has gone away," Holmes said at last. He called to Rosalie a few times, but nothing happened. "I think she has also gone away. Let us take a brief rest. Then we will try again."

During the break, Philip took Marie aside. "That was remarkable. I detected no deception. What did you make of it?"

"I agree. I really don't understand what happened. But, oh Philip, I wish I had taken your advice and not eaten so much at dinner. My stomach is starting to feel upset."

"I warned you. Do you want to go back to our bedroom?"

"No. I want to see what happens next. Besides, I think Lord Lytton would be offended if I simply left."

"Then here's an idea. Go to the kitchen area and see Mrs. Roberts. Cooks generally have a remedy for dyspepsia on hand."

"Good idea. I'll do just that."

Meanwhile, the other guests had dispersed into little groups, eager to discuss what they had witnessed during the séance. Lady Carey made her way across the Drawing Room to where her husband was seated. "I know he must have been making those rapping sounds and shaking the table himself, but I cannot say how on earth he managed it," Cora said, looking quite perplexed.

"Obviously, you were too distracted by the atmospherics to focus on what was really happening. It's the oldest tactic in the book: feint in one direction and attack in the other."

"Aye. So, when we resume, perhaps you'll keep watch for his maneuver and scout it out."

"Better still, why don't we take advantage of this break in the proceedings and slip away to our room? When this hocus pocus is going on, it's too dark in here to read."

"No, William. Better dig in and see it through. Remember what Miss Hickman advised. It's a performance, and the fact that it's well done is no reason to leave the theater."

In another part of the room, Lord Lytton, looking quite pleased with himself, conversed with Lord and Lady Henry Worthing. "Daphne," he asked, "I hope you were impressed by what occurred."

"I was indeed. I had expected little but got a lot."

"It was remarkable, dear Daffy," drawled Lord Henry, "how you entered into the spirit of the thing."

"Leaving your jeu d'esprit aside, Henry," Lytton responded, "did you not for a moment wonder whether Holmes had managed to penetrate the greatest mystery of all?"

"By no means. I may have an undeserved reputation as a cynic, but one would have to be truly a naif to accept that bit of legerdemain at face value."

"How do you mean, Henry?" Daphne asked, genuinely interested in her husband's opinion, as she sensed he was not, for once, just playing the hardened misanthrope.

"Just this. Earlier today, Lord Lytton, you complimented me on my capacious memory. Permit me to display another example of it. In the introduction to your excellent novel Zanoni, you gave an account of the old bookseller who had a shop in Covent Garden but who loved his books so well he could not bear to part with them, even going so far as to put off would-be buyers such as yourself. Anyone who has read Zanoni and remembers it as I do could have impersonated the old bookseller in the way we just witnessed."

"I must correct you once again, Lord Henry," said Lytton in a bantering tone. "Actually, I described your memory as imperfect, and you have now displayed another example of that imperfection. It's true that I wrote of the old bookseller in Zanoni. But nowhere in that work did I give his name. I only identified him by his initial 'D.' But tonight, we heard the actual name of the bookseller. No one could have gotten that from my book."

For once, Lord Henry was speechless, but Daphne came to her husband's defense. "But you must concede, Lord Lytton, that if you remember the bookseller's name, so might others. After all, he had his bookstore in a prominent place in town. Many others must have browsed there and might remember him."

"Possible, but unlikely. I wrote Zanoni a quarter century ago. I believe I mentioned in it that perhaps some readers would recall the old bookshop in Covent Garden. Even at that remote time, the bookshop had long since closed. There would be very few people around today who remember the place, and fewer still would recollect the proprietor's name. Certainly, Mr. Holmes, who was not yet born when the old bookseller went to his reward, could have had no knowledge of it."

"It is unlikely that anyone but yourself remembers the old bookseller by name," Lord Henry conceded, "but it is even more unlikely that Mr. Drotz just happened by for a chat."

✻✻✻

When Marie entered the servants' hall, Mrs. Roberts and two kitchen maids, who had been relaxing at the table, rose immediately to their feet. "Is there something you were needing, ma'am?" the cook asked.

Marie hesitated. "I wanted to thank you for that wonderful meal you prepared."

"Thank you, ma'am. You're very kind."

"The food was so good … I ate too much."

"Feeling a bit queasy now, are you?"

"I'm afraid so."

"It 'appens. It's the sauces, probably. Very rich. But never fear. I've got just the thing for that. Just wait right 'ere, please."

Mrs. Roberts went into a cupboard and emerged with a bottle. "Ginger beer. Just the thing to make you right as rain. I'll pour you a glass full."

"Thank you, Mrs. Roberts."

"That's all right, ma'am. Just sip it slowly now. That's the way. Wonderful stuff. 'Ow' is it?"

"Good. But a bit sharp."

"That's the ginger that does that. But it's good for what ails you. Sip it slow-like."

"Thanks again. I think I feel better already."

✵✵✵

When Marie returned to the Oak Drawing Room, the séance was ready to resume. "Here's our dear Marie," said Lytton. "Mr. Holmes, we're ready now to start again. James, the lights!"

Once again, it took some time, but Holmes succeeded in reaching Rosalie. This time, Rosalie rapped once for "yes" when asked if someone had a message for Gladys Hornell. The ensuing exchange, as recorded by Philip, was brief:

Q. You have a message for me?
A. Yes, Gladys.
Q. You know me well enough to address me by my Christian name?
A. I gave you that name.
Q. Oh, and what is, or was, your Christian name?
A. Lucrece. But your father called me Lottie.
Q. Mother!
A. Yes.
Q. What is your message, mother?
A. Be good to your husband!

At that, Mrs. Hornell burst into tears, and the conversation ended.

After about ten minutes of silence, Rosalie again rocked the table. This time, there was someone with a message for Philip. "What is your message for me?" he asked, somewhat bemused.

"W-A-R-N-I-N-G."

"Warning?" Philip repeated. "Who gives me warning?"

"M-O-N-T-Y."

"Monty!" When Philip shouted the name, Marie screamed in terror. She collapsed and slipped to the floor.

"James, light up the lamps," Lytton ordered. "I am sorry, Mr. Holmes, we must terminate the séance. Mrs. Deflorette is unwell."

Philip bent down and embraced her. "Marie, Marie, what is wrong, dear? Tell me what I can do."

"Philip, is Monty dead? Is he really dead?"

"I don't know, dear. Everything happened so fast. Is that what's troubling you?"

"Yes. No, not only that. My stomach. It's gotten much worse."

Jackson then came over to Lytton, who looked stricken as he watched Marie obviously in pain. "M'lord, I must inform you that Dr. Baker is here to check on your condition, as you instructed. He has been waiting in the Reception Hall until the séance could be completed. Do you wish him to examine you now?"

"Don't be a damn fool! Bring him in here at once! Immediately, you hear? Not to examine me but to look after Mrs. Deflorette. Don't you see she's ill?"

Dr. Baker was hurried into the room. He set down his medical bag and began to examine Marie. "Help her onto that sofa," he instructed James. After ascertaining her symptoms and checking her vital signs, he summoned Jackson to his side. "Is there an empty bedroom nearby where this lady may be taken?"

"Certainly, Dr. Baker. Shall I have one of the footmen take her there now?"

"Yes. Also, is there a reliable female servant who might assist me?"

"Let me see. There's Mrs. Pierce, the head housekeeper. And there's a parlor maid, Susan, a hardworking and intelligent young woman, who I believe would be of great help to you."

"Splendid. Have this Susan sent to that bedroom where Mrs. Deflorette is being taken. Then, have one of the other maids place some empty buckets there, as well as a large pitcher full of water."

"I'll see to it at once, doctor."

"Also, have one of the maids bring some towels, lots of them. Oh, and also a robe that might fit this young lady."

Once he had issued his instructions, Dr. Baker went over to have a word with Philip and Lord Lytton, both of whom had been anxiously watching the proceedings.

"I will now be going to the bedroom where Mrs. Deflorette is being taken. I promise to do my best for her. It may be a long night."

"May I go to her?" Philip asked.

"No, it's best for you to leave it to me for now. Try to get some rest if you can. This will take time, and I need to get started as soon as possible, getting it out of her system any way I can."

"But what is wrong with her doctor? Can't you tell me anything?"

"I hate to speak until I am certain. But I see Sir Robert Penrod standing over there. Lord Lytton, could you ask him to come here very quickly?"

Lytton did so. "I'm sorry your wife is not feeling well, Mr. Deflorette," Sir Robert said. "Lord Lytton, is there something you wish to tell me?"

"Dr. Baker wishes to speak with you."

"Yes, doctor?"

"Sir Robert, it is too soon for me to make a definite medical diagnosis. But, as you are Sheriff of this county, I feel it my duty to inform you that it is my preliminary opinion that Mrs. Deflorette has been poisoned and is in grave danger."

CHAPTER ELEVEN

A PERFECT CRIME?

"If the doctor's right in his suspicions, and for now we have to assume he is," Sir Robert observed, "that means a crime has taken place in this house tonight. Someone must begin the investigation. And I suppose it's up to me. But I really wish there were a police inspector here to handle it."

"There will be soon," Lytton said. "Colonel Fielding of the Detective Bureau will be arriving here in the morning. Meanwhile, carry on as best you can."

"Colonel Fielding? Arriving in the morning? How is that possible?"

"I will explain all that in due course. But right now, you must begin the investigation. A guest in this house may have attempted murder tonight. And he, or she, may well have succeeded."

"You're right, of course. Let us gather all the guests in this room as soon as we can. And also, please send for that Mrs. Pierce, the head housekeeper, along with another maid or two, and a footman."

Lytton called for Jackson, who saw to it that Sir Robert's orders were carried out promptly.

✳✳✳

Sir Robert Penrod faced the assembled guests. It struck him that this was not a typical set of suspects in a criminal case: before him stood a Baron, formerly an official in the government; the son of a Marquess and his wife; a War Office advisor and his wife; and a prominent journalist and his wife. Sir Robert whispered to Lytton: "Two are missing. That spiritualist and Mr. Deflorette."

"After Marie collapsed, I gave Mr. Holmes a pound note for a job well done and sent him on his way. As for Mr. Deflorette, he is devastated. I told him to remain in his room until he had recovered. It was disappointing to me that he is unable to face this crisis in a manly fashion."

"Disappointing, perhaps, but certainly understandable," said Sir Robert, visibly surprised by Lytton's attitude.

"Anyway, he certainly cannot be deemed a suspect," Lytton insisted.

"I'm not so sure. I've seen many cases of husbands murdering wives and wives murdering husbands. Many a time, the spouse is the first one suspected."

"Not this time."

"Very well, then, let's deal with the lot we have here." Sir Robert then cleared his throat and addressed the group gathered in the room. "As you know, ladies and gentlemen, Mrs. Deflorette is under medical care and may have been—it's a possibility anyway—deliberately poisoned. I regret to say that it is my duty to search each and every one of you. Mrs. Pierce will now lead you three ladies to another room and, assisted by a parlor maid, she will there perform a thorough search of each of you. I will myself, assisted by James, search the four gentlemen."

"Does this mean you consider me a suspect?" shouted Mrs. Hornell. "I refuse to be subjected to such an indignity."

"Don't you understand that a crime has been committed here, possibly murder?" said Daphne Worthing in a commanding voice. "You have a choice, madam. You can either go into the other room and be searched by Mrs. Pierce, or you can remain here and be searched by me on the spot. I assure you, I will be very thorough." Affecting an attitude of outraged dignity, Gladys Hornell followed Mrs. Pierce into the other room.

Then, Sir Robert turned to Jackson and gave him further instructions. "I want you to search all the guests' rooms and all other parts of the house where any of the guests might have spent some time this evening. Get an alert staff member to help you. We're looking for any container—bottle, jar, envelope, anything—that contains, or could have contained, any powder or liquid or anything else that might possibly be poison. If anything looks even half-way suspicious, bring it to me. And for God's sake, don't taste it!"

Sir Robert then conducted a meticulous search of the male guests but found nothing. Mrs. Pierce soon reported that her search of the three ladies had proved likewise futile. Finally, Jackson also returned empty-handed.

"What do we do now?" asked Lytton.

"I wish I knew," Sir Robert shook his head. "I don't think there's anything to be done until Colonel Fielding gets here. That reminds me: you were going to tell me how it is possible that he'll be arriving tomorrow morning."

Lytton took a moment to consider the matter.

"Let's go to my study. I will then tell you what you need to know."

Once they were settled in the study, Lytton showed Sir Robert the threatening note that Philip had kept to himself from the time it had been delivered in Torquay until he turned it over in the Knebworth Library. It was that threat, Lytton explained, that led him to send an urgent message to Colonel Fielding.

"This note makes it a virtual certainty this crime was premeditated," Sir Robert said with resignation. "I had been thinking, or rather hoping, that maybe she swallowed something by accident that made her sick, or perhaps she just had a bad case of dyspepsia. But it seems obvious, because of that note, that one of your guests brought along a poison—arsenic, I'm guessing—and put it in poor Mrs. Deflorette's food when no one was looking and then disposed of the evidence. As I think of it, the way that dinner was served, with everybody going back and forth to get a little of this and a little of that, it would have been easy for someone clever and diabolical enough to have done the deed with no one the wiser."

"If that's the case, the identity of the villain might never be disclosed."

"The so-called perfect crime. That's a possibility. At this point, I fear, it seems a probability. But I wonder if this paper, on which the would-be murderer wrote his threat, might give us some kind of clue."

"I had considered that potentiality myself," Lytton acknowledged.

"Any ideas about where it might have come from?"

"Yes. It was from a magazine that had published this poem celebrating the Cambridge boatmen."

"Cambridge, eh? That gives me an idea. It may well be that the one we're looking for might be a Cambridge man. Who else would have such a poem on hand?"

"That's a good point," Lytton agreed.

Sir Robert looked thoughtful. "I seem to recall that Lord Burnley was at Cambridge."

"As was Lord Henry Worthing."

"As were you as well."

"Yes, just a few years before you went there."

"That's true enough," Sir Robert conceded. "Of course, it would be a mistake to read too much into it. After all, anyone could have purchased this magazine. It doesn't prove anything."

"Perhaps not," Lytton said. "But for now, it's our only clue."

Both men remained silent for a good while, each hoping the other would have an idea. The silence was broken by the approach of Mrs. Hornell.

"May I speak with you gentlemen?" she said in an uncharacteristically deferential tone. "I have something of vital importance to tell you."

"Yes, Mrs. Hornell," said Sir Robert. "Tell us, by all means."

"I know who poisoned that poor girl."

Lytton and Sir Robert exchanged skeptical glances. But Sir Robert was well practiced at questioning witnesses. "Perhaps it would be best if you were to begin at the beginning," he advised.

"Certainly, Sir Robert. My husband and I were seated in the Banqueting Hall, listening to that girl's wonderful musical performance. Just after dinner was announced, I noticed that Worthing woman—I won't refer to her as 'lady' anything because she is decidedly not a lady—carrying two champagne glasses. What caught my attention was the odd way she was carrying the glasses. She carried the one in her left hand far out in front of her, as far away as possible from her own body, while she kept the one in her right hand close to her chest. She went over to the piano and pressed the poor girl to take the one glass—the one that had been in the left hand—and drink from it. The Worthing woman then smiled as she herself drank from the other glass, the one she was holding in her right hand. When they went on to dinner, the Worthing woman kept her glass and had it refilled several times during the meal. But Mrs. Deflorette left her glass behind and had nothing to drink during the meal. I believe the champagne she had been tricked into drinking was the only thing she had to drink all evening."

"Did you happen to notice what Mrs. Deflorette did with her glass after she drank the champagne?" Sir Robert asked.

"Let me think. Why, I believe she placed it on the piano. It may be there yet."

"Let us go see."

They went to the Banqueting Hall and, indeed, found a champagne glass on the piano. There was still some champagne left in it. At Sir Robert's request, Lytton sent for Jackson. When the butler arrived in the Banqueting Hall, Sir Robert handed him the champagne glass.

"Jackson, this glass may contain vital evidence. Be very careful not to spill it, nor to let anything else be put into the glass. It must be locked away somewhere safe, where no one can tamper with it in any way. Mrs. Hornell informs us it may contain the only thing Mrs. Deflorette had to drink all evening before she became ill."

Jackson assured the Sheriff he knew the perfect place to keep the glass. When Jackson took the glass away, Sir Robert sincerely thanked Mrs. Hornell for her timely assistance. "I only want to see justice served," she said with as much humility as she could manage and then returned to her bedroom.

A little later, Jackson sought out Sir Robert. "I have done as you asked, sir. The glass and its contents will be ready to be studied whenever you wish. But I must tell you that the champagne was not the only thing Mrs. Deflorette had to drink last evening."

Jackson then reported what Mrs. Roberts had told him about Marie's visit to the Servants' Hall. "Yes, I remember," said Lytton, "she had been off somewhere, and we had to delay resuming the séance until her return. I had wondered where she went, and now I know."

"I will need to speak with Mrs. Roberts right away. Is she still in the Servants' Hall?"

"Oh no, sir. She went to bed some time ago."

"I'm afraid, Jackson, you will have to rouse her and bring her to the Servants' Hall. We will meet you there."

"I trust you gentlemen don't believe there was anything wrong with the dinner," said a very worried Mrs. Roberts. "I'm so sorry that Mrs. Deflorette is ill. I 'ad supposed she just ate too much. It 'appens. But poison? Not possible. Everyone is very careful in my kitchen. I keep an eye on everything; you may be sure of that."

"Let me assure you, Mrs. Roberts," said the Sheriff, "no one is suggesting you did anything wrong. We know there was no poison in the food, at least there wasn't when it left your kitchen. None of the other guests was the least upset following the meal. I myself enjoyed the meal very much, and I feel fine, except for being very tired and wishing I were in my bed. What I wanted to ask you about was the drink you gave Mrs. Deflorette later that evening."

"Oh, that. Well, she came by 'ere and said she was feeling rather poorly. I took from the cupboard a bottle of ginger beer. I'll show it to you, just a moment." Mrs. Roberts stepped into the cupboard and returned with the ginger beer. "This 'ere is the very bottle from which I poured what she 'ad to drink. I'm truly sorry it did 'er no good, but I know it did 'er no 'arm either."

"Where is the glass from which she drank?"

"It should 'ave been washed and put away—but no, there it is, sitting on that table there. I can't be cross with Dottie for not getting to it. It was very late and there'd been so many dishes to wash."

"I'm afraid I will have to take this glass and the bottle as well. The contents might need to be tested. I doubt if there's anything wrong, but one must be thorough."

"Do not fret, Mrs. Roberts," said Lytton. "No one thinks you did anything but try to help. And I shall instruct Jackson in the morning to order more ginger beer."

Sir Robert and Lytton returned to the latter's study. "I suppose we should now call Lady Henry Worthing for cross-examination," the Sheriff said glumly.

"I would not put too much stock in what Gladys Hornell had to say," said Lytton sharply. "She's a spiteful woman. What possible reason could Lady Henry have for poisoning Marie? Oh, I realize you'll need to talk to her about the champagne glasses at some point. But it's very late now, nearly one o'clock, I see. I believe everyone else has gone to bed. Don't you think it can wait until morning? After all, a chemist can test what's in the glass, and that would answer the question one way or the other."

"True enough. It'll be a matter for the chemist, make no mistake. Besides, I'd prefer to let Colonel Fielding do whatever questioning of Lady Henry might be needed. She's such a fine young woman—oh, never mind, one can't be influenced by such considerations. Perhaps, you ought to go to bed yourself, Lord Lytton. I know this has turned out to be a dreadful day for you."

"Unspeakable. I know I should go to bed, but I'm too worried, too angry, too fearful to sleep. I'll stay up another hour or so, in case Dr. Baker has anything to report. Let's leave the study; I'll take you to one of the parlors that has some very comfortable chairs. If we have to sit up most of the night, at least we can do so in comparative comfort."

They had sat in the parlor more than two hours, sometimes dozing, when, at 3 a.m., Philip entered the room. He started to speak, but stopped, not wishing to waken the others. But his presence sufficed to startle Sir Robert from his sleep. "Is there any news?" the Sheriff said in an unintentionally loud voice.

"No news yet," said Philip, sounding calm but emotionally drained. "I spent most of the evening lying on the bed, weeping and praying, just weeping and praying. I guess it was about an hour ago that I pulled myself together and decided I must see Marie. I walked about and found the room where they had taken her. But, oh, the sounds coming from that room—and the smells—I could not go in. I did not want to see Marie like that. I did not want to be in the way and ...." His voice trailed away.

"We understand, dear boy," said Lytton, "It's best to leave it to the doctor. I feel certain he's doing what needs to be done, however unpleasant it may be. Dr. Baker is a good doctor. He's treated me for a long time. I know of none better."

"Why don't you rest yourself in one of these chairs and stay with us," suggested Sir Robert. "I doubt if you'd get much sleep in your bed anyway, and you really ought not be alone at a time like this."

Philip nodded and took a seat near the fireplace. Exhausted, he soon dozed off. The others slept on and off, through the hours of darkness.

Dawn came at last, providing just enough light to rouse the three men from their slumber. They sat up as they heard footsteps approaching from the hall in their direction. Could it be Dr. Baker at last, they wondered. But they saw in the morning twilight that it was Susan, the parlor maid, who had been assisting Dr. Baker. The tears streaming down Susan's face told them all they needed to know.

It was all over.

CHAPTER TWELVE

ENTER COLONEL FIELDING

Colonel Fielding made a formidable figure. He stood six feet one and weighed fifteen stone (210 pounds). Broad-shouldered and bald, he could easily be taken for a prize fighter or, perhaps, a bodyguard to some dignitary. Yet, in his work as the head of the Detective Bureau, he was thoroughly professional. His soft-spoken manner put at ease persons otherwise intimidated by his appearance. Yet, however polite he might be, people instinctively knew it would be most unwise to trifle with him.

Jackson greeted him when he arrived at Knebworth, accompanied by two other men whom he introduced as Sergeant Hooper and Officer Strawn.

"I wish to see Lord Lytton as soon as possible," said Colonel Fielding. "We are here at his urgent request concerning a death threat."

"I regret to inform you, Colonel, that the threat was fulfilled. A young woman was murdered here last night."

"Indeed? What was her name?"

"Marie Deflorette."

"Who was she?"

"She was the wife of Lord Lytton's private secretary. She was an American who played the piano admirably. Lord Lytton and all his guests feel absolutely heartbroken about what occurred. Permit me to add, I myself do so as well."

"Naturally, of course. How was she murdered?"

"As to that, I do not know. But I do believe poison was suspected. I can tell you that a bottle and two glasses from which she drank have been preserved for your inspection. Lord Lytton wishes you to undertake the investigation."

"Of course. Please show Officer Strawn where the bottle and the glasses are being kept. He will take charge of them. But first, let Lord Lytton know I have arrived. I wish to speak with him."

"Unfortunately, Lord Lytton is not yet up. He was awake most of the night, and I let him remain in bed later than usual. But, if I may make a suggestion, perhaps you might first interview Dr. Baker, who endeavored to save Ms. Deflorette's life. He wishes to return to his office to perform certain tests pertinent to the case but was persuaded to remain here awaiting your arrival. In the meanwhile, I shall look in on his Lordship."

"I will follow your suggestion, Mr. Jackson. By the way, you mentioned Lord Lytton's guests. Who are these guests?"

"There is Mr. Deflorette, the widower of the lady who was murdered. Sir Robert Penrod, who, as you know, is the High Sheriff of the County, dined here and then undertook the investigation, pending your arrival. Sir Robert is the one to thank for the preservation of the bottle and the two glasses. Lord Burnley is also a guest. Three couples are staying here as well."

"Thank you, Mr. Jackson. Now, please take me to Dr. Baker and Officer Strawn to the bottle and glasses."

✳✳✳

Dr. Baker was struggling to remain awake. He seemed quite relieved when Colonel Fielding entered the room and introduced himself.

"I thought you'd never get here, Colonel. What a terrible night it was. Doctors, I know, are supposed to become inured to matters of life and death, as, I assume, police detectives are as well. But not me; I realize now I'm not inured at all."

"Nor am I," said Colonel Fielding sympathetically, "and I hope never to become so. Now, Dr. Baker, can you tell me whether you have an opinion as to the cause of Mrs. Deflorette's death?"

"It's too soon to say. We need to do an autopsy. By the time of the Inquest, I expect to be able to answer that question to a reasonable degree of medical certainty."

"I appreciate your caution, Dr. Baker. But in order that I might put the investigation in the right direction, what would you hypothesize as the likely cause of death?"

"Poison. My initial examination, along with her report of her symptoms, strongly suggested that. My treatment largely focused on getting the poison out of her system, by purging her and inducing vomiting."

"If you had to make an educated guess, what poison do you think she ingested?"

"I suspect arsenic. I have suspected it all along. I'm going to perform the Marsh test today. That will tell us whether arsenic was in her system. I will let you know the result as soon as I can."

"I appreciate that. Let me ask you another question that also calls for an educated guess. Assuming it was arsenic, would you think it was a very large dose?"

"To that, I can make an educated guess with more assurance than I could in response to your other questions. I don't believe it could have been a very large dose. A large dose would have carried her off quickly. But from the time I first examined her until the time of her death, five hours, at least, had elapsed. And, of course, some time had passed between her being poisoned and my initial examination. Certainly, she fought hard for her life. I was able to take at least a brief medical history. She reported that she had been very sick a year or so ago. From her description, I suspect she had had a bout of pneumonia. It deprived her of what strength she had, and she was probably rather frail beforehand. It is entirely possible that a stronger, healthier person could have survived the amount of poison that was in her. But for her, even a relatively small amount was just too much."

"One final question, doctor. Do you have any theories about how the poison was put into her system?"

"I cannot speak to that. Perhaps Sir Robert Penrod has some theories along those lines, but I most certainly do not."

"Thank you, Dr. Baker. We will be back in touch soon."

✿✿✿

Soon afterward, Colonel Fielding was ushered into the study, where Lytton, clad in his dressing gown, awaited him.

"Nasty business, from what I hear," Colonel Fielding said, with characteristic understatement.

"One of the worst nights of my life," said Lytton. "But I'm glad you're here. You will discover the truth."

"I came here to discuss a death threat. And instead, I am investigating a murder. Any leads, as far as you know?"

"The death threat you reference is our only lead. That is, unless the bottle of ginger beer and the glass Marie used to drink it are found to contain poison, which I doubt. The same may be said about the glass from which she drank champagne."

"One of my men took possession of those items and will have them tested. Tell me about the death threat."

Lytton opened a desk drawer and took from it the envelope containing the threatening note and handed it to Colonel Fielding.

"Cold-hearted, whoever wrote this," Fielding remarked after he read the note. He then placed it into a portfolio he carried. "But it doesn't help us identify the killer."

"Perhaps not. But I think there's a possibility that Marie's murder may tie in with that other matter that we discussed when I last saw you."

"There you surprise me. I'd be very interested to know why you say that."

"The explanation will take some time. I would like Sir Robert Penrod to be present when we discuss it, if you have no objection."

"None. I think Sir Robert made a good start on the investigation."

"Also, I would like to have Philip Deflorette present as well. I feel he is entitled to know everything, and he may be able to provide some additional facts. That is, unless you feel that it would be indiscreet."

"Not at all. We always assume that whatever a statesman such as yourself knows, his private secretary knows as well."

"That's settled, then. Give me some time to get properly dressed. Also, we should confer in the library. There is more room, and it's more private. Why don't you have something to eat or drink while you're waiting? I can have Jackson arrange it, if you wish."

"No, thank you. What with one thing or another, I find I have no appetite."

Philip sat in the library looking lost. It seemed impossible to him that only two days had passed since he had conferred there with Lord Lytton. Now he was facing two law enforcement officers to discuss the murder of his beloved wife.

"Before we go any further, Mr. Deflorette," said Colonel Fielding, "I wish to express my most heartfelt condolences to you. While there is nothing anyone can say or do to ease your suffering, you have my personal assurance that we will bend every effort to bring those responsible to justice."

"Thank you."

"At this time, I understand Lord Lytton wishes to lay before us certain facts that might have some bearing on the case."

"Yes, I will address what I deem to be the salient facts, with your assistance, Colonel. I realize that you, and perhaps Sir Robert, may think I'm going far afield, but please bear with me.

"As we discussed earlier, Philip, when you began working for me, you found a letter from Gathorne Hardy, written while he was Home Secretary but received after the election results had removed him from that office."

"I remember. He had anticipated that eventuality and referred you to Colonel Fielding here."

"Yes. And I journeyed up to London and conferred with the Colonel just before Christmas. Perhaps, Colonel Fielding, you might set forth the substance of that conference."

"Certainly. I assume you gentlemen remember the deadly bombing of Clerkenwell Prison by the Fenian secret society in an effort to free one of their leaders.

We learned that members of that secret society had set up a safe house here in Hertfordshire. We wanted to make certain that all major public figures in the vicinity were aware of this peril."

"Please tell us what you can about how this information came to light," Lytton said in a hushed voice.

"A young Irishman informed us that he strongly suspected some friends he had made at a public house were Fenians. These friends talked a good deal, after downing a few pints, about the wrongs done to Ireland. This young man sensed they were feeling him out to see if he might join their cause."

Sir Robert interrupted the narrative. "I have no wish to learn things that might be dangerous to know," he cautioned. "Besides, I fail to see what bearing this has on the investigation we're about."

"Please hear us out," said Lytton. "We will endeavor to be discreet."

"I'll go on, then," said Colonel Fielding. "We advised the young man to remain friendly with these men but not to seem inquisitive or eager to join. The best thing would be to let them take the initiative. We set up a secure means for him to communicate to us any critical intelligence he might learn. All the while, we made allowances for the possibility he might be playing a double game, seeking to feed us lies to mislead us. Our trust in him was very limited as he had identified himself as Elias Carr, which we were sure was a pseudonym."

"Elias Carr?" Philip repeated. "That's odd. I had a friend in college by that name. It could not be the same person, but it's certainly quite a coincidence."

"Perhaps not," said Lytton.

"We did receive some significant intelligence from this fellow Carr," Colonel Fielding continued. "It was thanks to him that we were able to arrest one of the leaders of the conspiracy, a fellow called Fergus Thornton. We also learned from Carr that Thornton's comrades were planning to break him out of the jail in St. Albans, where he was being held pending trial. In other words, we suspected they were going to try to do here in Hertfordshire what they had done at Clerkenwell back in sixty-seven. We were hoping Carr might be able and willing to provide us with the details."

"All this is truly shocking to me," said Sir Robert.

"Indeed, it is," said Colonel Fielding, "and so is this. A few weeks ago, the body of a young man was found in the small town of Newton Abbot. In case you're not familiar with the place, Mr. Deflorette, it's a short distance from Torquay. This young man had been brutally murdered. There's not much crime in that part of the world, so the case attracted considerable interest in the Detective Bureau. No one in Newton Abbot seemed to know the young man, except his landlord, who knew only that he had recently begun renting a room from him. A search of the room turned up some papers indicating the young man's name was C. H. Hill, which we suspected was also false. Other papers we found there obviously belonged to someone who had served in the Navy of the Confederate States of America."

"That's a coincidence as well," said Philip. "I had another college friend who had also served in the Confederate Navy."

"But, consider this," said Colonel Fielding. "The last communication we had from this Elias Carr was that he was going to a meeting of the secret society to be held in Torquay. He was hoping then to learn the identities of some of their leaders. But he never reported anything further to us. Indeed, since the time C. H. Hill was found murdered, we have heard nothing at all from Elias Carr. He has simply disappeared."

Sir Robert clapped his hands together smartly. "I see where you're going with this. You believe that Carr and Hill were one and the same person."

"Wait a moment," said Philip, who had a sinking feeling in his stomach. "The real Elias Carr and I attended the college located in Chapel Hill, North Carolina. 'C. H. Hill' may be a pseudonym chosen by someone who had lived in Chapel Hill. If so, the murdered man may have attended the University of North

Carolina and served in the Confederate Navy during the war."

Lytton nodded vigorously. "You now understand my reaction when you told me the other day that a college friend of yours, who had served in the Confederate Navy, was seen on a number of occasions in Torquay. It was for that reason in particular that I sent an urgent message to Colonel Fielding to come here as soon as possible."

Philip bowed his head. "So, the man brutally murdered in some obscure seaside town was probably Monty Kelly. If I had any tears left, I would shed them now."

Colonel Fielding gently placed his hand on Philip's shoulder. "Thank you for the information you have provided. Perhaps we now have an inkling of the possible motive behind the murder in Newton Abbot, as well as the dreadful crime committed here last night. It will now be my duty to begin questioning some of the other guests. But there is no reason you should have to sit through all that. It will be disturbing to you, needlessly so. I have no wish to make your ordeal even worse than it already is. Please go somewhere to rest—perhaps to the patio. The fresh air will do you good."

"Thank you, Colonel Fielding. I believe I will follow that suggestion."

The Colonel and Lytton watched in silence as Philip unsteadily trudged out of the room. "He seems to have aged ten years overnight," Lytton remarked sadly. After a moment of reflection on the tragedy, Colonel Fielding turned his attention to the business at hand.

He made it plain that he saw little connection between Marie's murder and the death of the young man in Newton Abbot. "What we must do now is to follow up on all possible leads. Let's go to the Banqueting Hall and begin questioning the possible suspects. I'll have Sergeant Hooper notify all your guests to stand by in case we decide to interrogate them. I believe I'll begin with Gladys Hornell, the one who informed us about the champagne glass."

"I'm sure," said Lytton, "you will go by the book and follow all the proper procedures. But I must beg to be excused. I heard Mrs. Hornell's story yesterday. I prefer to return to my study."

"You're certainly free to do as you choose, Lord Lytton. I understand you do not wish to hear her statement a second time. But, of course, I haven't heard it at all."

"True, all too true. May I take with me to the study the threatening message I gave you earlier? I cannot shake the conviction that it has some meaning we have thus far overlooked. After all, it is the only evidence tied to the murderer himself."

Colonel Fielding removed the document from his portfolio and handed it back to Lytton. "Just be careful with it. We might need to show it to a jury someday."

Once Lytton had left the library, Colonel Fielding gave an update to Sir Robert. "Before questioning any of them—I don't know if I should call them guests, witnesses, or suspects—I wanted to get a bit more information about them. To do that, I'm having Officer Strawn go about the house, questioning the servants about what they may have seen or heard. Over the years, I've learned that people talk pretty freely around servants. It's almost as though they forget they're there. I'll have a good review of Strawn's notes before I question any of the 'guests' myself."

"I hope someone on the staff got the goods on Mrs. Hornell. Lytton's right about one thing: that woman's not worth listening to twice."

CHAPTER THIRTEEN

COLONEL FIELDING
TAKES CHARGE

Colonel Fielding managed to turn the spacious Banqueting Hall into an interrogation room. A table was set up in the center, with three chairs behind it, to be used by the Colonel and Sir Robert, along with Sergeant Hooper, who would be taking notes. Two chairs were positioned on the opposite side of the table for the use of the "witnesses."

Sir Robert Penrod looked puzzled. "I don't understand what you hope to accomplish with these interviews. After all, the chemist will tell us if there was poison in the champagne or in the ginger beer. And if there wasn't any in either, it must have been in the food. Unfortunately, I didn't think to have the plates checked before they were washed. Improbable as it seems, a lethal dose was put into the poor girl's food entirely unobserved by the nine other people who were dining there. At least, I have a suspicion that that's exactly what happened."

"I need hardly remind a barrister of your vast experience that a mere suspicion cannot support a conviction in court. Several vital facts remain to be discovered. First, we will need to know the actual cause of death. The autopsy will tell us that. If poison was the cause, as we suspect, we need to know the specific type employed. Dr. Baker was willing to speculate that it was arsenic. The Marsh test may confirm that. Or, perhaps, it may turn out to be some other type of poison. Once we know, we would need to find out which of the suspects, if any, had possession of that particular poison last night.

"The next question must be which suspect had an opportunity to use the poison to murder the victim. From what I've heard about how the dinner was carried on, I would say that at least ten people had the opportunity to put the poison into the victim's food. Finally, we would need to show what motivated the suspect to murder Mrs. Deflorette."

"You're right about the importance of identifying the motive, Colonel Fielding. I myself have stressed a lack of motive in a number of speeches to the jury." A satisfied expression came over Sir Robert's face as he recollected past triumphs.

Colonel Fielding resumed his analysis of the case. "It appears to me our greatest difficulty will be to prove that anyone in this house had poison in his possession last night. That is, assuming the tests of the champagne and the ginger beer come out negative. Jackson tells us that, to his knowledge, no arsenic is kept in the house. The gardener has some, but it's locked away."

"It sounds hopeless," Sir Robert said, "unless you're going to suspect the gardener."

"Not at this time. I believe we will have to try to prove possession by circumstantial evidence. As I said, there were at least ten people at the dinner who had the opportunity to tamper with the young lady's plate. If we eliminate you and Lord Lytton as suspects, that reduces it to eight people. And if we strike Mr. Deflorette from the list, that leaves us with seven. Those are the ones I wish to question. If we put the questions properly, one of the seven might slip up and reveal the missing motive. By any chance, Sir Robert, do you have a theory about which of the seven might have had a motive to murder Mrs. Deflorette?"

"Frankly, I have been pondering that issue, and nothing has come to mind. I believe six of the seven barely knew the girl. From what I understand, they had met her only once before. The only one who really knew her was Mark Hornell, but from my observation, they seemed very fond of each other."

"We will question him last, and his wife first. That will give him some time to worry, if he has reason to worry. By the way, how long after the dinner did Mrs. Deflorette first complain of being ill?"

"It was quite a while afterward. Let me think. I recall she collapsed during the séance."

Colonel Fielding raised an eyebrow. "Séance? I know nothing about any séance! Who was conducting this séance?"

"A charlatan called Daniel Holmes. Lord Lytton had arranged his appearance. When the séance ended so abruptly, due to Mrs. Deflorette's collapse, Holmes, with Lytton's approval, immediately left the premises before I had an opportunity to question him."

Colonel Fielding then addressed himself to Sergeant Hooper. "Please make a note that we will have this Daniel Holmes picked up for questioning. I expect you'll find that the branch of the Metropolitan Police that deals with fraud and the like will be very familiar with this fellow."

"Yes, Colonel."

"The séance struck me as a great example of fraud," Sir Robert remarked. "But all the participants seemed completely taken in by it."

"Just who were the participants?" Colonel Fielding asked.

"Aside from Holmes, there were seven others. I remember that particularly because they asked me to join them, as Holmes wanted to have eight people around the table. Of course, I flatly refused. Lord Henry Worthing then agreed to fill the spot. Let me see, there were Lord Henry and his wife, the Deflorettes, Mrs. Hornell, Lady Carey, and of course Lytton and Holmes. That makes eight."

"What about Sir William Carey, Mr. Hornell, and Lord Burnley?"

"Sir William and I remained in the Banqueting Hall, but both of us took seats far away from the séance table and, as it happened, far away from each other as well."

"And Mr. Hornell?"

"Oh, right. I forgot about him. Come to think of it, I don't know where he was. I seem to recall Lytton saying that Hornell was probably secluded somewhere, talking politics with Lord Burnley. But I don't know if that was really the case. Come to think of it, I don't recall seeing either of those gentlemen from the time the dinner broke up until I summoned them to be searched last night."

At this point, Officer Strawn entered the Banqueting Hall, carrying with him the notes he had made of his interviews with the servants. Colonel Fielding read them carefully, and, as he did so, a satisfied expression came over his face.

"We now have something to go on," he said. "Officer, please escort Mrs. Hornell to the witness chair."

✳✳✳

Once Gladys Hornell had taken her seat across the table, Colonel Fielding greeted her politely and asked her to tell him what she reported to Sir Robert the previous day. She repeated her account of Daphne Worthing handing a glass of champagne to Marie.

"But I don't quite understand what disturbed you about that. Did you actually see Lady Henry put anything into the champagne?"

"No, I did not. But I'm sure there was poison in it. May I explain why I came to that conclusion?"

"Please do so."

Gladys responded, showing considerable poise and self-assurance. "Whenever I carry two glasses of wine, intending to bring one to a friend and to drink the other myself, I hold them close together, one in each hand, so that my friend can select whichever one she wishes. And I would then drink from the one that remains. But the Worthing woman always kept the one glass in her left hand far in front of the other. It was obvious she wanted the poor American girl to take that glass and only that glass. Certainly, Mrs. Worthing would under no circumstances drink from that glass herself. And the reason for that became obvious when Mrs. Deflorette became so dreadfully ill." Gladys paused before adding in a whisper, "and soon the poor girl was dead."

"But the champagne was not the only thing Mrs. Deflorette had to drink that evening, was it?" asked Colonel Fielding.

"I believe it was. So far as I observed, she had no wine with dinner."

"But she did have tea earlier, did she not? I understand that she had tea with you, is that not so?"

"That's true. We enjoyed tea on the patio together."

"Who poured the tea?"

"I did. But I poured it in the normal way. And I had a cup from the same pot. I took one lump of sugar, and she took none." Gladys seemed to be enjoying herself.

"What did you two talk about at the tea table?"

"Oh, just the usual things. Gossip, I'm afraid. That's what ladies typically talk about, I'm ashamed to say. You gentlemen would be appalled if you knew some of the things that are said at teatime."

"Well, that's exactly what I'm asking you now. What things were said at teatime yesterday?"

"Now, let me think. I recall that she asked me—oh, I hate to tell you this, because it's like speaking ill of the dead—but if I must, I must. She was very interested in Lord Lytton's private life. Naturally, I had to say something. I must admit I did tell her that Lord Lytton has rather an unsavory reputation where women are concerned, and that gossip concerning his private life was being whispered about all over London. But I never mentioned any woman's name, I can assure you of that. Even so, I feel very guilty about saying even the little I did, right here, in his own home, after he so kindly invited us to spend the week with him. And now I'm repeating those remarks to you gentlemen. I implore you not to repeat what I said to Lord Lytton! He has been such a great friend to my husband, and I'd hate to have a foolish remark of mine ruin everything!"

"Speaking of remarks of yours," said Colonel Fielding in a calm, highly professional tone, "it is only fair to tell you that you were overheard telling Mrs. Deflorette that she should leave England. Why did you tell her that?"

Gladys was unfazed. "So, it sounds like someone had nothing better to do than to eavesdrop on us. Well, whoever it was, they got it all wrong. I believe that usually happens with busybodies who eavesdrop on others. In fact, Mrs. Deflorette told me that she was definitely planning to discuss with her husband whether they should return to America. I simply suggested that there are lots of other places they could go. For instance, I recall suggesting they might go to France. I don't know why I said that. Maybe it was because I believe her husband is of French ancestry. My husband and I often visit France. My husband, you know, is very well connected in political circles on both sides of the Channel. Did you know he once dined with Louis Philippe?"

"No, but that must have been interesting. And did you once send a note to the Deflorettes stating they should leave England?"

"Certainly not. Why should I? I only met her husband briefly, two or three times, when he worked for my husband. And I met her just the one time, yesterday. And it turned out to be the last day of her life." Gladys wiped a tear from the corner of her eye.

"I believe that's all the questions I have for now," Colonel Fielding said. "I want to thank you for telling us about the champagne. I assure you, the glass that you told us about will be taken to a chemist for analysis. If only more public-spirited citizens would be willing to step forward and tell us what they have seen, many more crimes would be solved than is now the case. Thank you, Mrs. Hornell. You may return now to the room from which you came."

"What did you make of that?" Sir Robert asked.

Colonel Fielding shrugged. "Just a piece of the puzzle. Now we should hear from Lady Henry. In fact, we need to hear from both Worthings. Officer Strawn, please fetch Lord and Lady Henry Worthing."

Once, the Worthings were seated before him, Colonel Fielding began to summarize what he had been told by Gladys Hornell, without disclosing his source. "An eyewitness has reported, Lady Henry, that you carried two glasses of champagne to the late Mrs. Deflorette following her concert here yesterday. One glass you held in your right hand and kept close to your body. But, in contrast, you held the other glass in your left hand, and as you walked, you kept your left arm outstretched."

"And you perceive something sinister in that?" remarked Lord Henry.

"Not at all," responded Colonel Fielding. "I'm only trying to ascertain the facts. I have drawn no conclusions as yet."

"I am happy to help you get the facts," Daphne stated. "I want you to catch whoever did this just as much as you do yourself. For what it's worth, I can confirm that I carried the champagne glasses in just the way you described."

"And what was your reason for doing so?"

"I was so impressed by Mrs. Deflorette's virtuoso performance on the piano. I could tell it tired her considerably. I felt sure that she could use a drink afterward. I knew I would! I also thought it might be a good way for us to get to know each other as friends if I brought it to her. So, I went to the footman in charge of the wine and asked him to pour two glasses of champagne. When he gave me the first one, I took it with my right hand—I am right-handed, after all—and immediately sipped a good bit of it. When he gave me the second glass, I took it with my left hand, as that was to be the glass I would offer to Mrs. Deflorette. That's all there was to it."

"I should tell you in fairness that the contents of the glass from which she drank are being analyzed by a chemist."

"That's as it should be. I am glad to find that you are so thorough. It gives me hope that you'll catch the murderer."

"I assure you, Lady Henry, we will do all we can." Colonel Fielding then turned to Lord Henry Worthing. "I now have some questions for you as well, Sir."

"Pray, proceed. I am accustomed to examinations."

"Lord Henry, I must tell you that you were overheard complaining to your wife that Philip Deflorette was to be offered a nomination in a by-election where you yourself had hoped to stand."

"Pray, continue."

"According to my source, you also said, and I quote, 'Why doesn't the fellow go back to his own country?' Did you, in fact, say that?"

"I have been most outrageously misquoted. What I actually said was, 'Why doesn't the damn fellow go back to his own damn country?' I'm sure, Colonel, that you'll forgive the strong language in the interest of keeping an accurate record."

"Well then, why did you say what you said?'

"For the reason you yourself just stated."

"You mean you were jealous?"

"Perhaps. My wife always says that I am too conceited to be jealous of anyone. This may have been my way of showing humility."

"Did you ever send Mr. Deflorette a note urging him to leave England?"

"You mean because of our supposed political rivalry? Permit me to remind you that I only learned of the rivalry, if that's what it was, yesterday afternoon. It would take me at least a week to compose a proper riposte, if such were needed. Do you suppose I would have dashed off a nasty note and had it delivered while he and I were staying under the same roof? My dear Colonel, I may be mettlesome in prose but not in person."

Colonel Fielding, for once, grew frustrated. "That's about all I have. Sir Robert, do you have any questions for this gentleman?"

"Yes, I do. By any chance, Lord Henry, are you familiar with a poem celebrating the Cambridge boatmen?"

"As a matter of fact, Sir Robert, I am. Curiously, this is the second time in two days I've been asked about this rather obscure bit of verse. Usually, if poetry is discussed in society, the conversation concerns the works of Tennyson or Browning, not a decade-old ditty by George Trevelyan. Next time I see old George, I must inform him of this sudden upsurge of interest in his work. I'm sure he'll be delighted."

"Did Lord Lytton tell you about this poem?"

"No, I told him. He somehow remembered some lines from it and asked me if I could identify the source. Thanks to my copious store of useless knowledge, I was able to slake his curiosity."

Sir Robert looked at Colonel Fielding and shrugged. The Colonel then undertook a different line of inquiry.

"I understand that both of you participated in a séance that was held here last night. What can you tell us about that?"

"It was, of course, a great humbug," responded Lord Henry. "I was a reluctant participant and most unwillingly responded to the call of duty. I am sure Sir Robert can attest to that fact. Still, I must admit that I did come to find the performance quite entertaining. I found it a particularly good show when they supposedly conjured up Mrs. Hornell's late mother, whereupon that nasty woman wept copious tears, though it was not clear whether she wept because her mother was dead or out of fear that she had come back to life."

"Actually," said Colonel Fielding softly, "I meant to ask whether anything occurred during that, er, performance, that might have had any bearing on the death of Mrs. Deflorette?"

"I don't know," answered Daphne, "but there was something peculiar about it. One of the messages, supposedly from the next world, upset Mrs. Deflorette very much, so much so that I thought for a moment it had caused her to faint. The message was some kind of warning. I don't remember who it was supposed to be from. Henry, do you recall? You usually remember everything."

"Yes, what you say about my memory is quite true. It's a curse. Now, what was it that you asked me?"

"What was the name of the person who supposedly sent Mr. Deflorette a warning from the Great Beyond?"

"Oh, yes, I remember. It was from someone called Monty."

"Yes, that's it," said Daphne. "It was Monty. Thank you, Henry."

Colonel Fielding was taken aback. "That was the same name that—well, never mind. Thank you both, Lord and Lady Henry. You may return now to the place where you were before."

Once they had left the room, Colonel Fielding quietly reviewed Sergeant Hooper's notes. Sir Robert looked discouraged. "So far, Colonel, I do not see that we're getting anywhere." Colonel Fielding was about to respond when he noticed that Jackson had entered the room and was trying to get his attention.

"Yes, Mr. Jackson? What is it?"

"Begging your pardon, Colonel Fielding, but Lord Lytton asks that you come to his study to speak with him. He also requests that you bring your portfolio with you when you come."

"This is quite inconvenient. We are in the middle of a series of interrogations. Please tell him I will join him when we're done."

"I am to tell you that the matter he wishes to discuss with you is most urgent."

"What is it that's so very urgent? Did he tell you that?"

"Yes, he did, Colonel. He instructed me to tell you that he now knows who murdered Marie Deflorette."

CHAPTER FOURTEEN

THE KNOT IS UNRAVELED

"I understand you have something of importance you wish to discuss with me," said Colonel Fielding as he entered Lytton's study.

"I do indeed, Colonel. Please be seated."

"Very well. You have my complete attention."

"Now that we know what happened," said Lytton cryptically, "all that remains is the matter of proof. We need evidence that will stand up in court."

"Evidence of what, exactly?"

"Ah, Colonel, I see you brought your portfolio with you. Excellent. Perchance, can you spare a blank sheet of that official-looking form you use to record evidence in cases? I need to make use of it."

Colonel Fielding hesitated a moment, then shrugged and handed over a sheet of the paper that had been requested. Lytton took up a pen and began writing on the paper.

"Thank you, Colonel, for your cooperation. Now, please be patient for about five more minutes. I'm a very fluent writer once I know what I wish to say. This might take a little longer than usual, as I am printing it with block letters lest the wrong people recognize my scrawl. Once I have this down on paper, I can then let you know what I have in mind." But the filling out of the form and the ensuing conversation took much longer than anticipated.

About half an hour later, Colonel Fielding, accompanied by Lord Lytton, returned to the Banqueting Hall. Both men looked pleased with themselves. The Colonel summoned the two policemen, who had taken advantage of their chief's absence to grab a snack from the kitchen.

"Officer Strawn, please bring a chair for Lord Lytton. He will participate in the next round of interrogation. Once you've done that, go and find Lord Burnley, and escort him here."

Lord Burnley looked quite uncomfortable as he sat across from the three interrogators.

"I don't really understand why you wish to question me. I know nothing about that poor girl's murder. I hardly knew her at all."

"I will appreciate your cooperation just the same," said Colonel Fielding. "I gather you kept a rather low profile throughout this proceeding. But it's important that we know where all the guests were and what they were doing last night. It's just a matter of routine."

"I understand. What do you want to know?"

"First of all, I have been told that you absented yourself from the séance that was conducted here last night. At the time it was taking place, where were you and what were you doing?"

"After dinner, Mark Hornell suggested we go off to some quiet corner to discuss certain matters of mutual interest. We found an empty parlor and remained there, having a stimulating conversation until it was time for bed. We only learned that Mrs. Deflorette had been taken ill when Sir Robert summoned us and had us searched."

"What was the substance of your conversation with Mr. Hornell?"

"Just politics."

"Can you tell us specifically what was discussed?"

"I prefer not to do so. This was a sensitive subject. It would cause me embarrassment if what I said were to be made public."

"I'm sorry, my Lord, but I must insist on an answer. This is a murder investigation. You have my personal assurance that what you tell us will remain confidential unless it is shown to be directly relevant to the subject of the investigation." Colonel Fielding glanced at each of his colleagues. "Can you gentlemen give Lord

Burnley the same assurance?" Both Lytton and Sir Robert Penrod responded in the affirmative.

"Very well, then," said Burnley. "This is what we discussed. I told Mark that Lord Derby's health is in serious decline, and he is not likely to live out the year. Accordingly, Lord Stanley will then inherit the title and move up to the House of Lords. In my opinion, he should then take over the leadership of the Tory party. The recent election proves Disraeli does not have either the prestige or, frankly, the character necessary to lead the party to victory in a national election. Mark disagreed. He believes Disraeli should remain the party's leader and that Stanley, once his father dies, would make a fine leader of the House of Lords and should serve as second in command of the party overall. But he should not supplant Disraeli until the latter decides it's time to step down. Well, that's the sum and substance of it, gentlemen. It did not take long to recapitulate, but it took hours for us to argue over all the possible ramifications.

"You yourself once served in government under Lord Derby, did you not?"

"I did indeed, Colonel, but it was a long time ago. I served as a junior minister in the first government that Lord Derby formed as Prime Minister. I have a great respect for him. He and his son have very different personalities, but both, I believe, are natural leaders."

"Just for the record, Lord Burnley, when did you last serve in any government office?"

"1852."

"Thank you, I believe you have answered my questions satisfactorily," said Colonel Fielding. "I appreciate that. You may now return to where you were. If you would be so kind, please ask Sir William Carey to come here next to answer some similarly routine questions. We are proceeding down the list alphabetically, you see."

Sir William Carey maintained his military posture as he settled into his chair. "Colonel Fielding, I am glad to meet you. I have heard much praise of your performance of your duties. How may I be of service to you?"

"As you no doubt are aware, I have taken charge of the investigation of the murder of Marie Deflorette. I need to ask you some questions. It's just a matter of routine."

Sir William shook his head. "I wish I could be of help. It was a dreadful thing that happened. But I know nothing about it."

"But you must understand," insisted Colonel Fielding, "every bit of information we can gather may prove useful. Even small details that may seem insignificant in and of themselves may prove quite helpful when put together with other bits of information gathered from other sources. You may be particularly helpful in this regard. After all, you no doubt have been trained to observe the small details. The capacity to be observant is a skill one must cultivate in your profession, is that not so?"

"You are correct, Colonel. I have indeed been trained in the manner you describe."

"I was wondering," Colonel Fielding asked in a friendly tone, "just when did you embark on a military career?"

"Just as soon as I was old enough to do so. In fact, I have been a soldier most of my life. I grew up near Liverpool, and as soon as I left school, I joined the 'Leather Hats.' I worked my way up thereafter. You know, I was thinking last night at dinner that most of the other men at the table had gone to Cambridge. They had a university education. But not me. I didn't need one. The army was my university."

"And you served well, not only in the forces, but in government as well, or so Sir Robert has told me."

"Very true. For years, I advised men in high office. That was how I came to know Lord Burnley. He was Under-Secretary of State for War and Colonies during Lord Derby's first ministry back in 1852, and he frequently consulted me in those days regarding military affairs. We've remained friends all these years since. And I'm sure, Lord Lytton, that you recall that, in 1858, when you were Secretary of State for the Colonies and I was working at the War Office, there was that crisis in South Africa. I briefed you about the military situation down there, remember that?"

Lytton nodded. "Certainly, I remember."

"Now with regard to the matter at hand," said Colonel Fielding rather smoothly, "did you observe anything suspicious during the dinner, anything that suggested to you that someone was trying to adulterate Mrs. Deflorette's food?"

"I saw nothing of the kind. I happened to be seated next to her, and I probably would have noticed had anything of the kind occurred."

"Then let's move on to another topic. Have you had occasion to visit Torquay in the past year?"

"That is quite a shift in topic, Colonel. But, yes, I've been there a few times. Lady Carey enjoys the sea air. It reminds her of her youth in North Berwick. Now, we never stay in Torquay the whole season, but we have spent a few days there, now and again."

"Do you recall the dates that you were there?"

"I really don't. Dates don't mean much to me these days. In my life, the dates spent on holiday are not very important."

"Well, Sir William, let me ask you this question. Are you aware of any death threats that were sent to Mr. Deflorette?"

"Certainly not. I don't know what you're talking about."

"Don't you?" Colonel Fielding then removed from his coat pocket the envelope containing the death threat and showed it to Sir William. "Do you recognize this envelope? As you can see, it is addressed to 'Mr. Deflorette.' I can tell you that it contains a note threatening the Deflorettes with death unless they leave England immediately. So, I ask you, Sir William, do you recognize this envelope?"

"Of course not. Even to ask me such a question is an insult. I will not stand for it, Sir."

"I am surprised you claim not to recognize it. Of course, when I first saw it this morning, I didn't recognize it either. But today, Lord Lytton held up the envelope to the light streaming in from his study window, and there, plain to see, was watermarked the date '1858.' And that jogged his memory, and he recognized that this was the type of envelope used by the War Office. And, as you just reminded us in your reminiscences, you were at the War Office in 1858."

"A watermark? A certain type of envelope? You think that is sufficient grounds to imply that I am somehow involved in murder? I realize, Mr. Fielding, that you find yourself in a difficult situation here. You've been called in to investigate a murder. It's a shocking crime: the senseless killing of a talented young woman. No doubt the press and public will take a great interest in the case. And obviously, you are desperate to catch the murderer. It will do great damage to your reputation should you fail. And so, you try to build a case against me based on a mere watermark? You'll be the laughingstock of England should you persist in this folly."

"Do you dispute, Sir William, that this is an envelope of the type used by the War Office back in 1858?" As Colonel Fielding asked that question, his confident expression conveyed the fact that he knew he could easily prove the envelope's provenance.

Before responding, Sir William made a show of leaning forward the more closely to examine the envelope. "Now that you've called my attention to it," he said in a casual tone, "I do see that it does resemble a War Office envelope. I don't dispute that. But, as you may know, many people work at the War Office. Many people worked there in 1858. Any one of them could have had such an envelope in his possession."

"That is true enough, Sir William. But how many of those people knew the Deflorettes? How many of them visited Torquay last winter? How many were visiting Knebworth this week? How many were seated next to Mrs. Deflorette at dinner last night?"

"You are obviously determined to convict somebody of this crime regardless of the lack of evidence," said Sir William defiantly. "No jury would return a conviction based on a watermark. I had thought you were a great detective. It turns out, you are as much a charlatan as that fellow Holmes, who was here last night. I have nothing more to say, except that I am very disappointed in you."

"Perhaps," said Colonel Fielding, "I can allay your disappointment by disclosing that I am not basing my inquiry merely on the watermark. In point of fact, the watermark merely confirmed what we already suspected." The Colonel then turned to the policeman seated to his left. "Sergeant Hooper, hand me that portfolio if you would, please." Once he had the portfolio in hand, Colonel Fielding busily searched through it for nearly a minute before finding the document he sought.

"Ah, here it is. It's a report from one of our undercover agents who infiltrated the Fenian secret society. You'll hear about it at your trial, so I might as well read it to you now:

"'I went out to the Red Lion again with Bill Dugan and Jim O'Keefe. They both got quite drunk, especially O'Keefe. When we left and crossed the street, we happened upon a man and a woman who were walking together. They were middle-aged, and both of them were quite fat. The man walked very erect, as if on parade. Jim whispered to me, "That's our leader." I think he was about to introduce me, but the man sort of growled at him and gestured for us to be on our way. The woman was more polite and bid us good day. From her voice, it was obvious she was Scottish. After we were some distance away, I asked Jim and Bill to tell me the name of the man, but they just looked at each other and shook their heads. So, I did not pursue the matter. I will keep you posted.'"

"A couple of foolish drunks," Sir William muttered, as if speaking just to himself.

"I am truly appalled," Lytton interjected in a voice that would have carried to the last row of a large theater. "Treason is distressing whenever it occurs. But for you, a man who served as a soldier of the Queen, to have betrayed his country is unthinkable. Even worse than that, for Cora to have involved herself is unwomanly and disgraceful. The consequences of what you've done will be too dreadful to describe."

"I agree with you, Lord Lytton," said Colonel Fielding. "I have worked on cases before that ended with a woman being hanged. It's a terrible sight."

"It will take a good, strong rope to hang this particular woman," observed Sergeant Hooper.

"Enough!" Sir William shouted. "Cora had nothing to do with any of it. She knew nothing about it. She still knows nothing about it."

"We have only your word for that," Colonel Fielding observed calmly. "Until this moment, you have not spoken a word of truth. If you wish us to believe you on this point, you must tell us the whole truth about the rest of it."

Sir William held his head in both his hands. "One must know when to accept defeat. I have lost this battle.

But Ireland will ultimately win her fight for freedom. If I am to be a martyr to the cause, so be it. A warrior should not die in bed anyway."

"Once we have taken you back to London," Colonel Fielding said softly, "we may have some questions for you about that so-called fight for freedom. But for now, we just want to know about the murder of Marie Deflorette. If you are candid with us on that subject, I, for my part at least, will accept the truthfulness of your exoneration of Lady Carey."

"Very well. I suppose that's fair under the circumstances. First of all, I want you to understand I did not intend to kill the girl. I'm not a monster. I acquired a supply of arsenic and kept it in a small envelope. I know about such things and felt certain the amount of it was only enough to make someone ill but not enough to cause death. I was willing to use it on either the husband or the wife. It just happened that I had the opportunity with her and not him. I figured if they disregarded my threat, a mild case of arsenic poisoning would hurry them out of the country."

Lord Lytton shook his head. "But why did you want them to leave England in the first place? You had only met them once. They had nothing to do with the discontent in Ireland. What did you have against them?"

"I did see them more than once. At least I saw her. It was in that big hotel in Torquay. I recognized her immediately and heard her playing the piano. I kept out of sight, behind a pillar, where I could watch her, but she couldn't see me. I soon realized what she was really doing there. She had arranged a rendezvous with that fellow, C. H. Hill, as he called himself. He had been palling around with O'Keefe and Dugan. They wanted to bring him into our group. But I distrusted him from the first. I suspected he might be a police informer. I knew that some of our plans were being found out. There were a couple of arrests that could not be explained unless the police were tipped off by somebody.

"When I saw Hill embracing that Deflorette woman, it all became clear to me. He was the informer. And she was his conduit to the police. He was telling her what he found out from drunken fools like O'Keefe, and she passed it along, probably to you, Colonel Fielding.

"Then, I thought about that dinner at Lord Burnley's. It seemed so strange that Lord Lytton would make some ne'er-do-well American his private secretary. I realized that the whole thing was an act, all rehearsed, to put the girl in a place where she could get secret intelligence from C. H. Hill, without his running the risk of being seen going to the police. I'm sure, Colonel Fielding, that you already knew about our meetings in Torquay. The fact that Lord Lytton was known to spend the winters there made it quite logical to insert one of your agents into his household."

"If that's what you believed, why did you bother sending the note to Mr. Deflorette?"

"I saw it as a kindness. They had no roots in this country. If I put a scare into them, they probably would run away. And there would be one less police informer to be dealt with in the way one deals with such people."

"Can you tell us," Lytton asked, "why you chose to write the threat on a page torn from a journal?"

"I remembered your promise to hold a reunion in the spring for everyone who had attended the dinner at Rockbridge House. I knew I might have to deal with the Deflorettes at that reunion. Well, one day, during the winter, my wife and I were visiting an old woman called Miss Hickman. She's a great friend of my wife's and also a great reader. She had books, magazines, and journals strewn about the house. I noticed one journal that had something in it about Cambridge. So, I nicked it, stuck it under my shirt, and took it away with me. A person built as I could hide the encyclopedia under his shirt and no one would notice. Anyway, Miss Hickman is short-sighted, and she never knew that I made off with this journal.

"As I said, I hoped the warning would make them flee. If that didn't work, I would have to employ other means. If I did so, it was important that someone else be suspected. I knew there would be at least three Cambridge men at the reunion dinner; I thought that the poem could serve as a false clue that might cause each of you to suspect the other. It seemed a good idea at the time. I thought I was being so clever. But I never even considered that the envelope might be recognized. That was stupid of me. I could easily have purchased a plain envelope. And here I just boasted about how I'm trained to give attention to the small details!"

"How did you actually put the arsenic in the victim's food unnoticed?" asked Colonel Fielding.

"Misdirection, of course. I kept an eye on the footman who was serving the wine. I waited for him to take a champagne bottle in hand. I knew that, when he popped it, everyone would turn to look in his direction. That was the moment the arsenic went into the veal sauce. I've always had quick hands. The empty envelope was back in my pocket, unseen by anyone. After dinner, I tossed it into a fire."

"It strikes me," observed an astonished Sir Robert Penrod, "that you describe everything with great detachment. You seem to have no remorse whatsoever."

"There is no room for remorse in war. The young lady's death is sad, but not sadder than the death of any other soldier. She made the decision to take part in the effort to suppress our movement to achieve freedom for Ireland. Her efforts helped to bring about the deaths of our people. She should have known the risks involved in what she chose to do."

"You scoffed a while ago about the significance of a mere watermark," said Lytton. "How could you kill someone based on nothing more than the fact that she embraced an old friend from her home country?"

"It seemed to me that the way I put everything together was the only way that it made any sense."

Colonel Fielding had heard enough. "We have taken down your confession, William Carey. Do you have anything else you wish to say, knowing that it may be used against you at your trial?"

"Only that I poisoned Mrs. Deflorette. I acted alone. No other person knew anything about it. Long live Ireland!"

"William Carey, you are under arrest for the murder of Marie Deflorette. Sergeant Hooper, Officer Strawn, secure the prisoner."

As the officers led the prisoner away, Colonel Fielding had one more thing to say. "I want you to contemplate this fact, Sir William, in the days and nights to come. Marie Deflorette was never an agent of ours. She knew nothing about it. You murdered an entirely innocent young woman."

Sir William shrugged. "I have only your word for that."

✫✫✫

In late May, Colonel Fielding returned to Knebworth to confer with Lytton. Sir Robert Penrod joined them for the discussion in Lytton's study.

"It all came to an end yesterday morning," Colonel Fielding said. "It might interest you to know that Sir William showed great courage as he stood on the gallows."

"Perhaps," replied Sir Robert, "but it may merely have been that he was resigned to his well-deserved fate. After all, courage is not a quality to be ascribed to a man who would murder a young woman by poisoning her."

"I suppose you're right," the Colonel responded. "I am relieved, in any event, that he got what he deserved. This was by no means an easy case to solve. I don't believe I could have done it without the help of you two gentlemen."

"You are overly generous, Colonel," said Sir Robert. "But I appreciate your kind words."

"I was wondering," Lytton asked, "how things went with Lady Carey?"

"Well, you will recall that after my men took Sir William into custody, we also brought Lady Carey to London for questioning. At first, she flatly refused to believe what we told her about her husband's confession. She kept repeating, 'It's all lies, all lies.' We permitted her to visit Sir William in the lock-up. He told her everything, and she was furious, saying she wished never to see him again. I understand she has now moved back to Scotland and is living with her sister somewhere near Edinburgh. I do believe that she had no connection with the Fenian conspirators."

"Yes, I'm sure you're right," said Sir Robert. "Even that report from your undercover agent that broke down Sir William did not really implicate her. All she did was bid some fellows goodbye. She said nothing that suggested she knew anything about their illegal activities."

"I wonder, Colonel Fielding," asked Lytton, "whether you were able to extract any information from Sir William concerning his fellow conspirators."

"No. I did try. But he refused to answer any questions on that subject. He often spoke of his devotion to the Irish cause. He even told me that, although he was well aware of the fate that awaited him, he felt relieved, even happy, that he no longer needed to wear a mask, as it were, and could speak freely about his beliefs. He had kept those beliefs mostly to himself for many years.

"In view of the death sentence, I had no leverage to use to get him to inform on others. He reminded me each time we talked that we had struck a bargain. I would not seek to prosecute his wife, and in return, he told me everything about the murder of Marie Deflorette. He kept his word, and I kept mine."

"You are indeed a man of honor, Colonel Fielding," said Lytton earnestly. "That is the highest compliment I can pay to anyone."

"Thank you, Lord Lytton. Still, we know that the way in which I extracted the confession from Sir William was not entirely honorable."

"What do you mean?" Sir Robert asked.

"It's curious," Lytton interjected, "that all along I had the feeling that the threatening note was the most important clue we possessed. I read and reread it, again and again, both the threat itself and the verse on the verso. Only reluctantly did I finally give up on finding the answer there. But when I took the envelope in hand and held it before the window, it was then that, both literally and figuratively, I saw the light."

"Yes," said Colonel Fielding, "I must congratulate you on recognizing that War Office envelope. That detail proved the key to the case."

"I feel obliged to state frankly that I disagree with both of you gentlemen on this point," said Sir Robert. "Colonel Fielding, I consider your handling of the matter to have been nothing short of brilliant." He then turned toward Lytton. "I must say, my friend, that I did not put much stock in that business about the envelope and the watermark. To be sure, you deserve credit for noticing it. I certainly missed it altogether, and so did the Colonel. But I don't believe it mattered very much.

"Oh, I understand your reasoning," continued Sir Robert. "The death threat was sent in an envelope that came from the War Office, that is true. It is also true that one might make a reasonable supposition that the actual murderer was the same person who had sent the threat. The murderer, therefore, might be someone connected to the War Office, someone who had served there and who was in this House at the time of the crime and therefore had the opportunity to poison Mrs. Deflorette. That narrowed it down to two possible suspects: Lord Burnley and Sir William Carey. But, of those two, Sir William was the only one who had worked in the War Office in 1858, the year that appeared in the watermark on the envelope. It no doubt seemed logical to you that, therefore, Sir William must have been the murderer. But, based on many years spent trying cases in court, I can assure you that no jury would ever have sent a man to the gallows based on so many inferences and assumptions, however logical they may be.

"No, Lord Lytton, I must give the palm to Colonel Fielding here. It was the evidence he uncovered, through the dangerous mission brilliantly performed by his undercover agent, that was the key to the case. That agent heard O'Keefe identify Sir William as the leader of the Fenian group. It was the prospect that the undercover agent would testify to that fact at his trial that forced Sir William's confession. And I feel quite confident in stating that the methods employed to obtain that confession were entirely honorable."

Lytton and Colonel Fielding exchanged significant glances. Lytton then said quietly, "Go ahead, Colonel."

"I will. Sir Robert, I must now make an admission that might dismay so ethical an ornament of the legal profession as yourself. These are the facts. We had no evidence linking Sir William with the Fenians. The report that I read to him here last month was composed just a few minutes earlier, in this very room, by none other than Lord Lytton. The only information I contributed to the report had been provided to me by Carr, or Hill, or, if you prefer, Monty Kelly. Whether Carr, Kelly, or Hill, the informant could not have given any evidence at Sir William's trial, as he was murdered last March. The only facts that I provided to Lord Lytton to assist him in composing the report were the names of the informant's pals, O'Keefe and Dugan, and the name of the pub where they liked to do their drinking. The rest of the report stemmed from the prolific imagination of one of the greatest novelists of our age. Someday, perhaps, I will be pleased to inform my grandchildren that I once collaborated with you, Lord Lytton, in composing a most advantageous work of fiction."

EPILOGUE

At Philip's request, Lytton arranged for Marie to be buried in a graveyard not far from Knebworth House. Philip said he believed Marie would have liked that.

Philip then made arrangements to travel on the first available ship sailing to America. He did not even wait for the execution of Sir William Carey to take place.

Philip soon settled in a small town just outside Wilmington, North Carolina. He found employment as a shopkeeper, a job that enabled him to earn a living while widening his circle of friends. All the while, he continued to prepare himself for the political career he had so long envisioned.

For several years following his return to America, he kept up a regular correspondence with Lord Lytton. In one letter, he expressed his regret that, while his education had given him a working knowledge of Latin, Greek, and French, it was deficient in respect to history and government, subjects with which he felt he should be conversant if he were ever to achieve his ambitions.

Lytton wrote back, suggesting a program of reading that could remedy this deficiency. He suggested the following books and authors: Sir Walter Scott, to learn about the days of King Richard the Lion-Heart; his own historical novel, The Last of the Barons, to learn about the Wars of the Roses; the works of James Froude, to learn about the Tudor era; and the essays of Lord Bolingbroke and Edmund Burke, as well as the Letters of Junius, to learn about the eighteenth century.

In December 1872, Philip wrote what would prove to be the last letter in the correspondence. It arrived in Torquay shortly after New Year's Day, and only weeks before Lytton's death there on January 18, 1873. In it, Philip wrote as follows:

I can now report that I am happier in my present work than I was when I first wrote to you about it. I am making many new friends, which is pleasant in and of itself, and helps me in becoming active in local politics.

I no longer think it feasible to plan on becoming a candidate for Congress in 1874. My target now is '76, but certainly no later than '78.

Meanwhile, I have been "improving" my education with the course of study you so kindly suggested to me. I very much enjoyed Ivanhoe and, of course, The Last of the Barons. On the other hand, I found Froude heavy going but stuck with it through the death of Henry VIII. I'll pick it up again someday. At present, I am reading The Letters of Junius and am delighted with it. There is much political wisdom contained therein, as well as polemics. I find the style very pleasing, although it is too old-fashioned to serve as a model. Anyone who spoke that way today would be deemed affected and pretentious.

Speaking of which, I was happy to learn that Lord Henry Worthing won his by-election to Parliament last summer. I know there was some friction between us at first, but that is (nearly) all forgotten now. After Marie's death, he and, especially, his wife Daphne were very kind to me. I wish them all the best.

At this season, I often think back on my last Christmas with Marie, four years ago. I no longer berate myself about what I might have done differently. One cannot live life that way. Marie lived her life looking forward, her eyes focused on the future, even as she venerated the past. Unafraid, she did the things she wanted to do. I no longer mourn her loss so much as I rejoice in the time we had together, including even the time we spent at Knebworth House.

Yours faithfully, Philip Deflorette

A NOTE ON SOURCES

Murder at Knebworth is a work of fiction. Most of the characters are purely imaginary, although, to be sure, some are based on, or at least inspired by, actual people, including of course, Lord Lytton himself (about whom I will have more to say below).

The fictional characters, Philip and Marie Deflorette, were inspired by two actual people: Louis de Rosset (1840-1875) and his wife Marie Finley de Rosset (1844-1870). Louis de Rosset came from Wilmington, North Carolina, served as an agent of the Confederate States of America, and became private secretary to Lord Lytton before returning to America. Marie de Rosset originally came from Charleston, South Carolina, where she married Louis at the age of 18. She was a talented musician and died in England. The de Rossets had a daughter, Gabrielle de Rosset (1863-1936), who, after her marriage, became Gabrielle Waddell.

It must be stressed, however, that while Louis and Marie de Rosset inspired two of the leading characters in this book, the story told herein is not their story. Anyone interested in the actual lives of Louis and Marie de Rosset is urged to read the very interesting and superbly researched article by Anna Koivusalo entitled, "'Nothing to Lose & Everything to Gain': Louis and Marie de Rosset's Intimate Friendship with Edward Bulwer Lytton," in Australasian Journal of Victorian Studies, vol. 26, no. 1 (2022), pp. 25-41.

Another helpful source for this subject was an article published by Gabrielle De R. Waddell, entitled "Reminiscences and Letters of Bulwer-Lytton," published in *The Century Magazine*, vol. 88, pp. 469-472 (July 1914). One might add that there is some information concerning Gabrielle Waddell (and her mother) in the Pulitzer Prize-winning book *Wilmington's Lie*, by David Zucchino, published in 2020.

As for Edward Bulwer-Lytton, First Baron Lytton of Knebworth (1803-1873), the representation of him in this novel may seem idealized but was intended at least partially to portray aspects of his career and personality. He wrote twenty-seven novels, about eight plays, a history of Athens, and many volumes of essays and poetry. He served in the House of Commons for a quarter century and in the House of Lords for about six years. He also served in the Cabinet as Colonial

Secretary. Among his many works, the following were referenced, directly or indirectly, in this book:

The Last Days of Pompeii—1834; *Zanoni*—1842; *The Last of the Barons*—1843; *King Arthur*—1848 & Revised Edition 1870; *Harold, The Last of the Saxons*—1848; *The Caxtons*—1849; *My Novel*—1853; *The Haunted and the Haunters*—1857; *What Will He Do With It*—1858; *A Strange Story*—1862; *The Odes and Epodes of Horace*—1869; *The Coming Race*—1870; and *The Parisians*—1873. (The latter was an unfinished novel, published posthumously; Anna Koivusalo indicated that *The Parisians* included a character that was based on Marie de Rosset.)

Information about Lord Lytton may be found in two full-length biographies, one by the Second Earl of Lytton (published in 1913) and the other by Leslie Mitchell (published in 2003). One might also consult a fine short biography by Sibylla Jane Flower. Many scholars have written specialized studies of aspects of Lytton's life and writings. Among those whose work may be consulted are Marie Mulvey-Roberts, Henry Cobbold, C. Nelson Stewart, Lillian Nayder, Philip Rand, Joachim Mathieu, and the late Allan Christensen, to name just a few.

Information about Knebworth House and Gardens was found in *Knebworth House—Home of the Lytton family since 1492*, a guidebook that lists no author, but which I believe was written by the late David, Lord Cobbold. Also very helpful was the following article: "E. H.-J."

[Lady Elizabeth Hills-Johnes], "Recollections of a Visit to Sir Edward Bulwer Lytton at Knebworth in 1857," *Blackwood's Magazine*, vol. 177, pp. 15-25, (January, 1905). The memoir written by Gabrielle Waddell, mentioned above, was also helpful on this topic.

ABOUT THE AUTHOR

Charles Snyder was born and raised in Boston, Massachusetts, where he graduated from Boston University before attending graduate school at the University of Virginia to study the history of England. During his studies there, he wrote a thesis about Edward Bulwer-Lytton, a nineteenth century novelist, playwright, poet, and politician. Knebworth House, Bulwer-Lytton's estate in Hertfordshire, England, still exists and is open to the public.

Charles went on to obtain his law degree from the University of Georgia and practiced law for over forty years, including six years as a staff attorney for the Federal Election Commission in Washington, DC, and the remaining years in Savannah.

Charles and his wife, Sylvia, currently live in Savannah, Georgia. They enjoy cozy mystery movies and books. *Murder at Knebworth* is a result of their love of the genre and Charles' earlier study of Bulwer-Lytton.